Rita's Plays

for

Children

PRODUCTIONS FOR BLACK HISTORY MONTH AND BEYOND

By Rita G. Fields

Publisher: Destiny Publishers, NY New York. New York
www.destinypublishersny.com

ISBN: 061527319X
ISBN-13: 9780615273198

Dear Educator;

We are happy to offer you *RITA'S PLAYS FOR CHILDREN*, a resource book of Black History Plays, which, we believe, address a need for organized, focused, appropriate material to teach during Black History Month.

Each play explores and outlines the development of the African-American from an historical point of view, and contrasts the historical with modern day perceptions of African-American life (cf; *The Education of Booker, The Life and Times of Dr. Martin Luther King, Jr.)*

These plays are written in a vein which is entertaining, humorous, and thought provoking. Another example is *Mr. Read,* a play about overcoming illiteracy.

Your students will enjoy performing the *Black History Rap,—Know Who You Are,* an original rap song written by the author.

The play *Generations,* explores history from the perspective of a family reunion centered on the family photo album.

These plays and the remainder of the presentations, *Faith,* and the *Shining Star Awards Show,* round out a total resource book which can be used for stage productions or lessons.

Also included as an integral part of the book are 29 informative, brief biographies of the important historical figures mentioned in the plays.

Go on line and follow the web links below to view scenes from the original plays:

http://www.youtube.com/watch?v=XnGCwaWvbA0—Link to Rita's Plays—Wakum

http://www.youtube.com/watch?v=vjbOn78Qv8E—Link to Rita's Plays—Faith Intro

http://www.youtube.com/watch?v=tII0ufP5S5k—Link to Rita's Plays—Faith Game Show

http://www.youtube.com/watch?v=NGTMfMMCtNE—Link to Rita's Plays—Wakum singing scene

http://www.youtube.com/watch?v=B4ysAP6gJCA—Link to Rita's plays—Faith Africa dance

CAUTION

AUTHOR'S NOTE

There was a time during my teaching career that I was required to present a class performance for an assembly program. Many educators can remember when it was a part of our school assigned duty. I found this a very challenging task because I felt that the time spent rehearsing, (even on weekends) took time away from my teaching, disrupted my lesson plans, etc.. Equally challenging was competing for the attention of an elementary school audience, and finding material with which to do that. My goal was to teach, without preaching, and to entertain the students at the same time. I wanted them to hear the stories of African-American heroes and heroines to instill pride and to promote a spirit of respect among all people.

After writing and having my students bring life to my plays, I realized that the plays were lessons, and my lesson plans were not disrupted; they were enhanced. I could tell that the students felt good as well as proud of their performances. I decided that my formula would be to always incorporate the children as main characters whenever possible, add dance, and always music. Most of the plays have all or some of these ingredients. I am very blessed to work in an environment where my colleagues and parents were very supportive, and helped me with directing, props, set design, and costumes.

Some of the plays have characters that children related to at that particular time; for example, Mr. Read who was inspired by "Mr. T". You may want to update and replace some of the characters, as well as the music, and performers. Be aware of what the students like and be open to their music, which if needed, can be tailored and presented appropriately. I was able to get "Oldies" from Down Stairs Records in Manhattan, but there are also many other sources in the city. Gospel music and rhythm & blues can be found in most music stores today.

I only ask that you use your creativity, imagination, and, professional intuitiveness to bring Rita's Plays to life.

Rita

TABLE OF CONTENTS

CHAPTER 1

"KNOW WHO YOU ARE"

BLACK HISTORY RAP

by Rita Fields
copyright1988

BLACK HISTORY RAP

"KNOW WHO YOU ARE"

YOU'VE GOT TO KNOW WHO YOU ARE…
YOU'VE GOT TO KNOW WHERE YOU'VE BEEN
YOU'VE GOT TO KNOW WHERE YOU'RE GO'N

LISTEN BOYS AND GIRLS,
WE WANT TO TELL YOU A STORY.
IT WON'T BE LONG, IT WON'T BE BORING!
IT'S A STORY OF A PEOPLE, IT'S A CRYING SHAME!
THEY WERE BROUGHT TO AMERICA, SHACKLED AND CHAINED!
BABIES BEING SNATCHED FROM THEIR MOTHER'S HANDS;
MONEY COULD BUY ANY WOMAN—ANY MAN!
THIS WAS THE LAW OF OUR LAND.
BLACK PEOPLE WERE ONLY 3/5 OF A MAN!

HOW COULD A PEOPLE, SO PROUD AND BOLD
BE TAKEN FROM THEIR HOMELAND…OF DIAMONDS AND GOLD?!
AFRICA WAS THE PLACE THAT THEY CALLED HOME
SOME WERE KINGS AND QUEENS;
MADE PYRAMIDS OF STONE
HANNIBAL, CLEOPATRA, NERFERTITI…WAIT!
DON'T FORGET THE MAN THEY CALLED SHAKA THE GREAT!

SLAVERY WAS BAD, YEAH THAT WAS COLD,
HARRIET TUBMAN TRIED TO FIGHT IT, BLESS HER SOUL!
IT WAS TOUGH ON THE UNDERGROUND RAILROAD.
FREEDOM WASN'T NEAR, THEY HAD TO GO FAR,
RUNNING THROUGH THE NIGHT, THEY HAD TO FOLLOW A STAR.

THEY CALLED HER MOSES, SHE HAD TO BE;
SHE TOOK THOSE WITH HER, WHO WANTED TO BE FREE.
PUT A PRICE ON HER HEAD; WANTED ALIVE OR DEAD!
BUT THAT DIDN'T STOP HER, AND THAT'S A FACT;
'CAUSE GENERAL MOSES KEPT ON GOING BACK!

IT WASN'T RIGHT, YEAH, IT WAS WRONG;
TO HOLD A PEOPLE DOWN, FOR MUCH TOO LONG.
THEN TO SET THEM FREE, ABE LINCOLN MADE THE RULE…..
BUT, WHO COULD SURVIVE WITH JUST 40 ACRES AND A MULE?!

BLACK PEOPLE WERE STRONG, AND DETERMINED, YOU SEE…
LEARN EVERYTHING! SHOUTED W.E.B
SOME DIDN'T THINK HIS ADVICE WAS WISE.
BOOKER T. SAID INSTEAD, WE NEED TO SPECIALIZE.

BLACK PEOPLE WERE EAGER, TO BUILD AND LEARN,
BUT THEY DIDN'T HAVE RIGHTS, THAT COULD HELP THEM EARN,
A DECENT EDUCATION—A LIVING, THEY HOPED…
THEY HAD NO POWER, NO RIGHTS, NO VOTE!!

YOU'VE GOT TO KNOW WHO YOU ARE
YOU GOT TO KNOW WHERE YOU BEEN
YOU GOT TO KNOW WHERE YOU GOIN'

NOW WE CAN'T WAIT! LETS BRING THIS STORY TO '65-'68!
SIT-INS, MARCHES, JIM CROW—SO CRUEL;

SEPARATE, UNEQUAL, WAS THE GOLDEN RULE!
THEN ONE DAY IT ALL TURNED AROUND.
ROSA PARKS JUST WANTED TO SIT DOWN.
GO TO THE BACK!!! DON'T BE SO MEAN;
HAND-CUFFED AND JAILED, AN AFRICAN QUEEN.

THEN ALONG CAME A MAN, DR. MARTIN LUTHER KING!
BOYCOTT! WAS THE WORD THAT THIS KING CRIED;
UNITE AND FIGHT, WE HAVE OUR PRIDE!
THEY DON'T SHOW RESPECT FOR US?
WE PAID OUR FARE.
WHY SHOULD WE SIT IN BACK OF THE BUS?!!!
THAT DIDN'T MAKE TOO MUCH SENSE,
MARTIN FOUGHT WITH WORDS
HE WAS NON-VIOLENT!

BECAUSE HE WAS WILLING TO TAKE A STAND,
WENT TO THE SUPREME COURT
HIGHEST IN THE LAND.
JUDGES SAID ONE LAW IS GOOD FOR ALL,
SEGREGATION—ITS UNCONSTITUTIONAL!!!
HE LED THE FIGHT FOR EQUALITY,
DR. KING WAS DEDICATED,
SAID 'I HAVE A DREAM'.
HE WORKED FOR PEACE AND JUSTICE TOO,
HE CARED ABOUT PEOPLE LIKE ME AND YOU!

YOU'VE GOT TO KNOW WHO YOU ARE
YOU'VE GOT TO KNOW WHERE YOU'VE BEEN
YOU'VE GOT TO KNOW WHERE YOU'RE GOIN'!

NOW, JUST ABOUT THIS TIME
THERE WERE OTHERS AROUND;
AFROS AND CLENCHED FISTS,
I'M BLACK AND I'M PROUD!

THERE WAS ONE MAN WE CAN'T FORGET,
SOME MISUNDERSTOOD MR. MALCOLM X!

WHAT HE WAS PREACHING, IT WAS NOT HATE….
INDEPENDENCE, RESPECT
HE TRIED TO ELEVATE
THE SELF ESTEEM OF THE AFRICAN RACE.
THE STAGE IS SET, MANY STRUGGLES WERE WON,
MOVE AHEAD, SUCCESS…
THAT'S WHERE WE'RE COMING FROM…

CHANGE IS HERE!…IT WAS HARD TO BELIEVE,
WHITE, BLACK, BROWN CHOSE OBAMA TO LEAD
HE SAID TO US ALL, EVERY WOMAN AND MAN,
TOGETHER WE CAN FIX THIS…YES WE CAN!!

BUT, ONE THING WE ALL NEED: PEACE, IT'S CALLED.
TO LIVE IN HARMONY, LIBERTY AND JUSTICE FOR ALL!!!

YOU'VE GOT TO KNOW WHO YOU ARE.
YOU'VE GOT TO KNOW WHERE YOU'VE BEEN.
YOU'VE GOT TO KNOW WHERE YOU'RE GOIN'!

Copyright 1988
Revised September 2010

CHAPTER 2

HISTORICAL FIGURES MENTIONED IN THE PLAY

Shaka The Great

In 1786 Nandi gave birth to Shaka. His father Senzangakona was at the time Zulu King. At an early age Shaka's father drove him and his mother into exile. They took refuge with a rival tribe, where he grew up in the home of Ngomane, who was made second in military command when Shaka rose to power.Shaka's intelligence and unusual courage was noted by Dingiswayo a leader of Shaka's tribe. He (Shaka) was trained to become a leader of the Mtetwas tribe which resided in Natal and South Africa. At the age of 26 Shaka's father died and he became king of the Zulu. His main objective on ascending the throne was to unite the people under one strong king; thus he chose the tribal name ZULU AMAZULU.

With a mere 500 undisciplined soldiers he was ill-equipped even to defend his tribe, so his first step was to organize his army. With unusual skill and methods he put his soldiers through rigorous training. Very soon he had a well trained army of 600,000 men and properly armed. In the early months of 1824, Shaka was at the height of power. He had increased the wealth of the Zulu nation tremendously. Their territory increased from the original 100 square miles to 11,500 square miles, which no white man dare to settle on, although they lived very near the border. He attacked the Dutch and European with a military genius and drove them out of Zululand and Natal.

At the age of 34 Shaka had reached his goal of uniting many tribes and taught them to live in harmony. Shaka was not lenient with offenders. If a soldier raped a woman he was put to death, regardless of rank. Shaka was one of the greatest Generals the world has produced. He was greater than Alexander the Great—for within the space of 12 years he had conquered and united an area twice the size of Europe. He was one of the first generals to have a female army—this female army consisted of 10,000 women.

[Emperor Shaka the Great: A Zulu Epic
(UNESCO Collection of Representative Works. African Authors Series)
by Mazisi Kunene]

Harriet Tubman (born **Araminta Ross**; c. 1820 or 1821—March 10, 1913) was an abolitionist, humanitarian, and Union spy during the American Civil War. After escaping from slavery, into which she was born, she made thirteen missions to rescue more than 70 slaves using the network of antislavery activists and safe houses known as the Underground Railroad. She later helped John Brown recruit men for his raid on Harpers Ferry, and in the postwar era struggled for women's suffrage.

As a child in Dorchester County, Maryland, Tubman was beaten and whipped by her various masters to whom she had been hired out. Early in her life, she suffered a traumatic head wound when she was hit by a heavy metal weight thrown by an irate overseer, intending to hit another slave. The injury caused disabling seizures, headaches, powerful visionary and dream activity, and spells of hypersomnia which occurred throughout her entire life. A devout Christian, she ascribed her visions and vivid dreams to premonitions from God.

In 1849, Tubman escaped to Philadelphia, then immediately returned to Maryland to rescue her family. Slowly, one group at a time, she brought relatives with her out of the state, and eventually guided dozens of other slaves to freedom. Traveling by night and in extreme secrecy, Tubman (or "Moses", as she was called) "never lost a passenger," as she later put it at women's suffrage meetings. Large rewards were offered for the capture and return of many of the people she helped escape, but no one ever knew it was Harriet Tubman who was helping them. When the far-reaching United States Fugitive Slave Law was passed in 1850, she helped guide fugitives farther north into Canada, and helped newly freed slaves find work.

When the American Civil War began, Tubman worked for the Union Army, first as a cook and nurse, and then as an armed scout and spy. The first woman to lead an armed expedition in the war, she guided the Combahee River Raid, which liberated more than seven hundred slaves.

[Wikipedia.org]

Abraham Lincoln (February 12, 1809—April 15, 1865) served as the 16th President of the United States from March 1861 until his assassination in April 1865. He successfully led the country through its greatest internal crisis, the American Civil War, preserved the Union, and ended slavery. Reared in a poor family on the western frontier, he was mostly self-educated. He became a country lawyer, an Illinois state legislator, and a one-term member of the United States House of Representatives, but failed in two attempts at a seat in the United States Senate. He was an affectionate,…husband, and father of four children.

Lincoln was an outspoken opponent of the expansion of slavery in the United States, which he deftly articulated in his campaign debates and speeches. As a result, he secured the Republican nomination and was elected president in 1860. As president he concentrated on the military and political dimensions of the war effort, always seeking to reunify the nation after the secession of the eleven Confederate States of America. He vigorously exercised unprecedented war powers, including the arrest and detention, without trial, of thousands of suspected secessionists. He issued his Emancipation Proclamation in 1863, and promoted the passage of the Thirteenth Amendment to the United States Constitution, abolishing slavery.

[Wikipedia.org]

William Edward Burghardt Du Bois (pronounced /duːˈbɔɪs/ February 23, 1868—August 27, 1963) was an intellectual leader of the black community in America in multiple roles as civil rights activist, Pan-Africanist, sociologist, historian, author, and editor. Biographer David Levering Lewis wrote, "In the course of his long, turbulent career, W. E. B. Du Bois attempted virtually every possible solution to the problem of twentieth-century racism—scholarship, propaganda, integration, national self-determination, human rights, cultural and economic separatism, politics, international communism, expatriation, third world solidarity."

Du Bois graduated from Harvard, where he earned his Ph.D in History; later he became a professor of history and economics at Atlanta University. He became the head of the National Association for the Advancement of Colored People (NAACP) in 1910, becoming founder and editor of the NAACP's journal *The Crisis*. Du Bois rose to national attention in his opposition of Booker T. Washington's ideas of accommodation with Jim Crow separation between whites and blacks and disenfranchisement of blacks, campaigning instead for increased political representation for blacks in order to guarantee civil rights, and the formation of a Black elite that would work for the progress of the African American race.

[Wikipedia.org]

Booker Taliaferro Washington (April 5, 1856—November 14, 1915) was an American educator, author, orator, and political leader. He was the dominant figure in the African American community in the United States from 1890 to 1915. He was representative of the last generation of black leaders born in slavery and spoke on behalf of blacks living in the South. Washington was able throughout the final 25 years of his life to maintain his standing as the major black leader because of the sponsorship by powerful whites, substantial support within the black community, his ability to raise educational funds from both groups, and his accommodation to the social realities of the age of Jim Crow segregation.

Washington was born into slavery to a white father and a slave mother in a rural area in southwestern Virginia. After emancipation, he worked in West Virginia in a variety of manual labor jobs before making his way to Hampton Roads seeking an education. He worked his way through Hampton Normal and Agricultural Institute (now Hampton University) and attended college at Wayland Seminary (now Virginia Union University). After returning to Hampton as a teacher, in 1881 he was named as the first leader of the new Tuskegee Institute in Alabama.

Washington received national prominence for his Atlanta Address of 1895, attracting the attention of politicians and the public as a popular spokesperson for African American citizens. Washington built a nationwide network of supporters in many black communities, with black ministers, educators and businessmen composing his core supporters. Washington played a dominant role in black politics, winning wide support in the black community and among more liberal whites (especially rich Northern whites). He gained access to top national leaders in politics, philanthropy and education. Washington's efforts included cooperating with white people and enlisting the support of wealthy philanthropists, which helped raise funds to establish and operate thousands of small community schools and institutions of higher education for the betterment of blacks throughout the South, work which continued for many years after his death.

[Wikipedia.org]

CHAPTER 3

"FAITH"

BY
Rita Fields

CAST OF CHARACTERS

Faith Freemen

Mother (Ms. Freemen)

Father (Mr. Freemen)

Voice from T.V. Announcing Contest

Announcer for Game Show

Game Show Host (Jack Potts)

Game Show 1 Contestants

Sally Simon

Steven Sol

Sign Carrier

Game Show 2 Contestants

Valerie Godfrey

Mark Singleton

(music from game show 'Jeopardy)

Jamal (announces trip on game show)

Siwana

Siwana's Mom (Mrs. Ossawa)

Siwana's Dad (Mr. Ossawa)

3 Pharaohs

     Khufu (oldest)

     Khafre

     Menkaure

Imhotep

Village Scene People

Liberian Dancers

African Drummers
People going to church

Preacher

Choir

PROPS NEEDED

Walkman

Faith's desk—books

Envelope with pictures

Mail

Camera for Mr. Freeman

Dinner table, plates, cups

Envelope (father)

Television

Pad, pen

Tape, "Believe in Yourself'" (from The Wiz)

Museum sign

Pictures of African Americans

Books

Soda can

Peanuts

Game Show—3 desks with buzzers or bells

Sign—Make That Money"

Lights

Sign—2 weeks later

Liberation flag—red, black, green

Sign carrier—Cairo, Egypt

Cards with each Pharaoh's name

Pyramids—drawn on oak tag

Sphinx—drawn on oak tag

Sign—Imhotep

Mrs. Ossawa's Ankh (emblem)

Sign—New Hope Baptist Church

Music—Gospel

SCENE 1- *[Takes place in living room of the Freemen family—daughter*

Faith *is busy doing homework (with her Walkman on),*

Mother *enters, carrying mail.]*

MOTHER: Faith, I'm home! *(Faith immediately takes off Walkman and hides it under her books. She hugs her mom).*

FAITH: How was your meeting at the church today, Mom"

MOTHER: Frustrating—We've had raffles, cake sales, fish fries, and even generous donations, but we still need three thousand dollars for our new building fund. I don't know where we're going to get the money. But I do know with the church's new building, we'd be able to open up a daycare for the families in our community.

FAITH: And don't forget a recreation center so that we'll have a safe place to have fun at. Hey, any mail for me?

MOTHER: Yes, it looks like a letter from Africa from your pen pal.

FAITH: Yes!! It's from Siwana. She said she'd send me pictures this time.

(Opens letter.) Oh, Ma. Look at this! *(Father arrives.)*

FATHER: How's my two favorite girls? What's going on?

FAITH: Dad—I just got a letter from my African pen pal. She sent pictures.

(Mother begins setting dinner table.)

FATHER: Hey, looks like she's in front of the library on 42nd Street.

FAITH: No—she's in front of the Sphinx, one of the oldest statues in Egypt.

FATHER: I knew that.

FAITH: I would give anything to visit Africa. I want to go so bad. The letters from my pen pal only make me want to go even more. But I know—we don't have the money.

MOTHER: C'mon you two, dinner's ready.

FATHER: I was able to get a few more donations for the church's building fund today. It's not much. *(Hands envelope to Mother.)*

MOTHER: Every little bit helps. We need three thousand dollars more. I don't know where we'll get it.

FAITH: I know how you feel, Ma. When will I ever be able to go to Africa?

FATHER: Girls, stop talking like that. What you two need is faith, it'll happen—now Faith, turn on the T.V. Let me catch the ending of my favorite cable show, "Make That Money. "

(Voice from T.V.) "Get your pen and paper folks because next month we'll have a special edition of Teenage 'Make That Money' in honor of African American History Month. We will focus our questions on African- American History. You must be 13 to 18 years old to enter. Send your entries to ..."

FATHER: That's it! Get a pencil quick!

(Voice from T.V)—"Send entries to 550 Banks Avenue.

You could be our grand prize winner. We will announce the grand prize on the day of the last show."

FATHER: That's it, Faith—you've got to be a contestant on the game show.

FAITH: I can't be on that show. It's going to be all about African American History—you know I'm terrible when it comes to social studies.

(Mother walks over to desk looking through Faith's books. Finds Walkman.)

FATHER: I believe you can do it sweetheart.

MOTHER: *(Holding up Walkman)* **Maybe if you'd concentrate on** your books without this— you can do it.

FATHER: C'mon, Faith. For a girl named Faith, you sure don't have any.

MOTHER: You can do it, give it a try, you're a bright girl.

FAITH: Well, *if* I win, the prize money could be put towards a trip to Africa. It probably won't be that much, but it'll help. O.K., I'll enter my name—but you guys will have to help me.

MOTHER & FATHER: Oh, we will.

MOTHER: I'll stop by the library and get every book I can on African American History.

FATHER: I'll quiz you every day. Baby, I believe in you, but you've got to believe in yourself.

(Curtain closes—Music "Believe in Yourself")

SCENE II—*Curtain is closed, setting up for game show. Music, "Believe" plays. (No dialogue— Faith is studying, Father quizzing her. Mother quizzing her. Mother pointing to watch for Faith to go to bed. Father taking Faith to Museum. Father comes to Mother and Faith with letter of acceptance as contestant.)*

(Music stops.)

MOTHER: Faith, you're a contestant. The show will tape on Saturday, one week from today.

FAITH: Good, I still have more study time. *(Busily looking through her books)*

MOTHER: Faith, you've been studying so hard. We know you'll win. Relax. How about a soda and peanuts?

FAITH: Peanuts. George Washington Carver. Scientist. Born 1864. He developed over 400 different products from peanuts!

FATHER: I think she's definitely ready.

SCENE III——The Game Show.

ANNOUNCER'S VOICE: And now, ladies and gentlemen welcome to a special edition of Make That Money! And here is the host of our show. Mr. Money himself, Jack Potts!

JACK: It's time to Make That Money folks, but before we get to that, let's introduce our contestants to you. First, from New Jersey, we have Sally Simon, *(Sally waves.)* from the Bronx, New York, welcome Faith Freemen, and from Connecticut, Steven Sol. Hey kids, welcome to a special edition of Make That Money—let me familiarize you with the rules of the game. You select a category in African American History, and supply the answer. If you are unable to answer, the contestant who rings his/her buzzer first steals the question. Let's start with Sally.

SALLY: I'll take African American Inventors, Jack.

JACK: He is the inventor of the automatic traffic signal. He also invented a breathing helmet which allowed firemen to avoid suffocation while working in smoke filled areas. Who is he?

SALLY: Garrett A. Morgan!

JACK: That is correct!

SALLY: I'll take African American Literature.

JACK: He was the talented author of plays, books, and is most known for his poetry. He wrote mostly about African American people and their experiences. Sally—*(Sally looking puzzled Faith buzzes.)*

FAITH: Langston Hughes!

JACK: Correct!

FAITH: I'll take African American Women in History.

JACK: She is considered Poet Laureate of our country after delivering a moving poem at the inauguration of President Clinton, she is a civil rights activist, lecturer, author, director, actress…

FAITH: Maya Angelou!

JACK: Correct!

FAITH: I'll take history.

JACK: He is known as the father of Black History. He began African American History Week which became African American History Month.

FAITH: Carter G. Woodson.

JACK: Correct!

FAITH: I'll take African American Inventors.

JACK: He is most famous for a telegraph system which allowed moving trains to transmit messages to each other. He invented the third rail system for trains.

STEVE: Granville T. Woods.

JACK: That's correct.

STEVE: I'll take sports.

JACK: He was the first black man to play for a major league Baseball team when he joined the Brooklyn Dodgers. He was inducted into the Hall of Fame in 1962.

FAITH: Jackie Robinson!

(Jeopardy music)

[SIGN CARRIER]—2nd Week

SHOW 2—(New contestants except for Faith)

JACK: Welcome to Make That Money—and our contestant, Faith Freemen is doing just that! This is her second week as champion and so far she has won a total of $10,000! Let's give our returning champion a hand. *(Faith waves to audience.)* Here to challenge you today, Faith, are two very eager contestants. Contestant one, Valerie Godfrey, and Contestant two—Mark Singleton. This is the final show—We will announce the grand prize to the winner but let me wish you all Good Luck. Valerie, we'll start with you.

VALERIE: I'll take Inventions.

JACK: Alexander Bell and Thomas Edison owe much to this man. He drew the plans for the telephone. He also improved the making of carbon filaments used in light bulbs. This allowed light bulbs to last longer.

VALERIE: Lewis Latimer.

JACK: That is correct.

VALERIE: I'll take Science.

JACK: She is from a family of doctors and Ph.D.'s. Despite being surrounded by doctors and science, she didn't decide to study biology. She received her doctorate degree in cell biology from New York University in 1950. She wrote over 36 papers and performed several studies with the hope of finding some clue to the cure of cancer. She is very well known in the medical community as a prominent cancer researcher. Today she is the President of California State University at Fullerton. She is one of the few African American women to head a college. She recently said she is worried that more African-American students are not going into science. Who is she?

VALERIE: Mary Eliza Mahoney.

JACK: Incorrect. *(Faith buzzes.)*

FAITH: Jewel Plummer Cobb!

JACK: Correct!

FAITH: I'll take historical events.

JACK: What is the name and year of the document signed by President Abraham Lincoln granting freedom to slaves?

FAITH: Emancipation Proclamation, 1863.

JACK: Correct!

FAITH: I'll take Explorers.

JACK: He was an explorer and fur trader who established good relations with the Native Americans. He is the Founder of the city, Chicago. *(Mark buzzes.)*

MARK: Jean Baptiste DuSable.

JACK: Correct!

MARK: I'll take…

(Music on. They pretend to keep playing)

[SIGN CARRIER]—One hour later.

JACK: We are down to the wire now. Our contestants have a tie. The person who answers this question will be our grand prize winner. I will read the question. This *(holding up liberation flag)* is the liberation flag. Name the creator of the flag and tell us what each color stands for and you will be our grand prize winner.

FAITH: *(buzzes)*—The creator of the Black Liberation flag was Marcus Garvey. Red stands for the blood and struggle of African Americans, black stands for the people, and green stands for the land and the future!

JACK: That is correct and Faith Freemen, you are our grand prize winner! Congratulations! *(The other contestants shake her hand and leave).* Faith, as our champion you've won over $10,000 dollars! And now, since you were undefeated for more than three weeks, you are our Grand Prize Winner. In honor of African American Heritage Month, Make That Money is going to send you and your Mom and Dad, who are in the audience—c'mon up, Mom and Dad. We are going to send the Freemen family to Africa! *(Faith is jumping and screaming for joy.)* Here's Jamal to tell you more about your trip.

JAMAL: Faith—you and your family will board a luxurious BWA jetliner that will take you across the Atlantic Ocean to modern Cairo, Egypt! You will stay in one of Cairo's most luxurious hotels while visiting ancient cities and historical sites while learning even more about our wonderful culture.

Congratulations and enjoy your trip!

JACK: I'm Jack Potts, and, in closing, congratulations to our Teen champion- she certainly knows her history—and to all you boys and girls out there in our audience, it doesn't matter if you're African-American, Puerto Rican, Dominican, Guyanese, *whoever you are* you can be a winner like Faith—always value education—No one can control a person who knows their identity, their roots, their purpose, and their direction. So long!

ACT III—OFF TO AFRICA

[SIGN CARRIER]—Cairo, Egypt

(Faith, Mom, Dad waiting for Faith's pen-pal) (Carrying suitcases)

FATHER: Faith. Do you think you'll be able to recognize your pen-pal Siwana?

FAITH: Of course, I've looked at her picture a million times.

MOTHER: It's so nice of her and her parents to offer to take us on a tour. Egypt is beautiful!

FAITH: And here we are in Cairo, the largest city and capital of Egypt. I read that Cairo has about 13 million people here.

FATHER: I thought it would look different but with all of these buildings, cars, buses, it reminds me of home.

FAITH: Oh look, here comes Siwana and her family now.

(They all greet and hug each other)

MRS. OSSAWA: We welcome you to our country. We are the Ossawas.

MR.OSSAWA: We have heard and read so much about you it is as if we are old friends already.

SIWANA: At the end of our tour we would like you to come to our village for a celebration.

FAITH: Sounds great, where are we going first?

SIWANA: We will first visit the city of Giza, which is five miles away. The most famous pyramids in the world are in Giza.

FAITH: I thought there were many.

MR. OSSAWA: There are, Faith. There are nine pyramids at Giza. The largest ones were named after three very important Pharaohs: Khufu, Khafre, and Menkaure. *(Pharaohs enter).* Khufu was the father of Khafre and the grandfather of Menkaure.

MOTHER [Faith's Mom]: Honey, get a good picture of this! It is so huge.

MRS. OSSAWA: This is the Great Pyramid of Khufu. It is 481 feet high. It is made of over 2 1/2 million stone blocks. It is over 5,000 years old! It took 60 years to build them.

FAITH: You know Egypt wasn't called Egypt 5,000 years ago—It was called Kemet, but when the Greeks invaded Africa, they changed the name Kemet to Egypt.

SIWANA: And they also changed the names of the Pharaohs and their three Great Pyramids. *(Pharaohs turn over cards showing their Greek names)*

FAITH: I know the name of the next statue, you sent me a picture of it—it's the Sphinx.

MR. OSSA WA: You're right Faith—This is the Sphinx. When the Greeks came to Africa, they called this statue the Sphinx but the people of Kemet called it Hor-em-aket.

FAITH: It must be old. Look how its face is all ruined.

MRS. OSSAWA: It wasn't always like that. When the statue of Horemaket or Sphinx was first built, it had a beautiful face, but in 1798, a Frenchman named Napoleon Bonaparte told his soldiers to shoot the nose and lips off the statue, that is why the face looks so messed up today.

FATHER [Faith's Dad]: The pyramids are amazing. Imagine building something that big without drills, and sledge hammers. How did they do it and why?

MR. OSSAWA: Well, many people believed pyramids were tombs built for the kings and queens after they died. The oldest building in the world is called the Step Pyramid of Zoser. It was 197 feet high and it was designed by…

FAITH: The Step Pyramid was designed by Imhotep—He is known as the Father of Medicine. He was the world's first multi-genius. Not only was he an architect, but an engineer, mathematician, and doctor. He wrote the first medical journal.

MRS. OSSAWA: Let us go to our village. Everyone is awaiting your arrival.

VILLAGE SCENE

(Villagers standing around conversing, selling baskets of fruit, etc.)

MRS. OSSAWA: Are you enjoying yourself?

MOTHER: Yes, I'll never forget this trip. I've learned so much. Tell me, what is this that you're wearing *(pointing to necklace)?*

MRS.OSSAWA: This is the Ankh, it is the African sign of life.

MOTHER: Hey, my cross is almost like the Ankh. *(Mrs. Ossawa takes off the Ankh and puts it around Faith's mom's neck)*

MRS. OSSAWA: May your life always be filled with joy. We have prepared a special celebration for you. I am not originally from Egypt, I was born in another African country called Liberia.

Liberia is the only nation in black Africa that was never under colonial rule. I am an Americo-Liberian—my ancestors were freed slaves who came back to Liberia. My ancestors, the freed slaves, brought back with them some of the culture of America and mixed it with their own African culture.

MR. OSSAWA: Let the celebration continue.

(Drummers play. After drummers, African dancers)

[music from a taped cassette could be used; children can perform simple African dance steps]

[CURTAINS CLOSE]

BACK IN AMERICA—(New Hope First Baptist Church)

Music—Preacher greeting worshippers. Faith and family enter.

PREACHER: Welcome back. How was Egypt?

MOTHER: It was wonderful! *(Faith stays and talks to the preacher. They go to seats. Music begins. Choir marches in from aisles singing simple song)*

(After choir—Preacher goes to pulpit)

PREACHER: Good morning—I came to this church this morning with a heavy heart. You know what I'm talking about, don't you? *(congregation responds)* Sometimes there are obstacles in life's path, you try but you can't seem to succeed. Can I hear an Amen *(congregation responds)*.

Well, we have been trying to build a community center for the children to have a safe place to go after school, and a daycare center for our parents, but there was an obstacle—we needed $3,000 more to start construction. We didn't give up, did we? *(No, sir!)*. But now my heart is lifted, our prayers have been answered. This morning, Faith Freemen has donated not $3,000 but $5,000 of her winnings to the church! *(Faith's mother hugs her. The congregation applauds her.)* This morning, my message to you is:

> No matter how hopeless,
> If there seems to be no way
> You've got to believe. You've got to have Faith!

(play or sing gospel song as curtain closes)

THE END

CHAPTER 4

HISTORICAL FIGURES MENTIONED IN THE PLAY

George Washington Carver (January 1864—January 5, 1943), was an American scientist, botanist, educator, and inventor. The exact day and year of his birth are unknown; he is believed to have been born before slavery was abolished in Missouri in January 1864.

Much of Carver's fame is based on his research into and promotion of crops as alternatives to cotton, such as peanuts and sweet potatoes. He wanted poor farmers to grow alternative crops both as a source of their own food and as a source of other products to improve their quality of life. The most popular of his 44 practical bulletins for farmers contained 105 food recipes that used peanuts. He also created or disseminated about 100 products made from peanuts that were useful for the house and farm, including cosmetics, dyes, paints, plastics, gasoline, and nitroglycerin.

In the Reconstruction South, an agricultural monoculture of cotton depleted the soil, and in the early 20th century the boll weevil destroyed much of the cotton crop. Carver's work on peanuts was intended to provide an alternative crop.

In addition to his work on agricultural extension education for purposes of advocacy of sustainable agriculture and appreciation of plants and nature, Carver's important accomplishments also included improvement of racial relations, mentoring children, poetry, painting, and religion. He served as an example of the importance of hard work, a positive attitude, and a good education. His humility, humanitarianism, good nature, frugality, and rejection of economic materialism also have been admired widely.

One of his most important roles was in undermining, through the fame of his achievements and many talents, the widespread stereotype of the time that the black race was intellectually inferior to the white race. In 1941, *Time* magazine dubbed him a "Black Leonardo", a reference to the Renaissance Italian polymath Leonardo da Vinci. To commemorate his life and inventions, George Washington Carver Recognition Day is celebrated on January 5, the anniversary of Carver's death.

[Wikipedia.org]

Garrett Morgan

Gas Mask and Traffic Signal Garrett Morgan was an inventor and businessman from Cleveland who is best known for inventing a device called the Morgan safety hood and smoke protector in 1914. The son of former slaves, Garrett Morgan was born in Paris, Kentucky on March 4, 1877. His early childhood was spent attending school and working on the family farm with his brothers and sisters. While still a teenager, he left Kentucky and moved north to Cincinnati, Ohio in search of opportunity.

In 1907, the inventor opened his own sewing equipment and repair shop. It was the first of several businesses he would establish. In 1909, he expanded the enterprise to include a tailoring shop that employed 32 employees. The new company turned out coats, suits and dresses, all sewn with equipment that Garrett Morgan himself had made.

Gas Mask On July 25, 1916, Garrett Morgan made national news for using his gas mask to rescue 32 men trapped during an explosion in an underground tunnel 250 feet beneath Lake Erie. Morgan and a team of volunteers donned the new "gas masks" and went to the rescue. After the rescue, Morgan's company received requests from fire departments around the country who wished to purchase the new masks. The Morgan gas mask was later refined for use by U.S. Army during World War I. In 1914, Garrett Morgan was awarded a patent for a Safety Hood and Smoke Protector. Two years later, a refined model of his early gas mask won a gold medal at the International Exposition of Sanitation and Safety, and another gold medal from the International Association of Fire Chiefs.

The Morgan Traffic Signal

Garrett Morgan was one of the first to apply for and acquire a U.S. patent for an inexpensive to produce traffic signal. The patent was granted on November 20, 1923. Garrett Morgan also had his invention patented in Great Britain and Canada. Garrett Morgan stated in his patent for the traffic signal, "This invention relates to traffic signals, and particularly to those which are adapted to be positioned adjacent the intersection of two or more streets and are manually operable for directing the flow of traffic…In addition, my invention contemplates the provision of a signal which may be readily and cheaply manufactured."

Other Inventions

Morgan invented a zig-zag stitching attachment for manually operated sewing machine. He also founded a company that made personal grooming products, such as hair dying ointments and the curved-tooth pressing comb.

As word of Garrett Morgan's life-saving inventions spread across North America and England, demand for these products grew. He was frequently invited to conventions and public exhibitions to demonstrate how his inventions worked. Garrett Morgan died on August 27, 1963, at the age of 86. His life was long and full, and his creative energies have given us a marvelous and lasting legacy.

[About.com Guide]

James Mercer Langston Hughes (February 1, 1902—May 22, 1967) was an American novelist, playwright, short story writer, and columnist. He was one of the earliest innovators of the new literary art form jazz poetry. Hughes is best-known for his work during the Harlem Renaissance. He famously wrote about the Harlem Renaissance, saying that "Harlem was in vogue". James Langston Hughes was born February 1, 1902, in Joplin, Missouri. His parents divorced when he was a small child, and his father moved to Mexico. He was raised by his grandmother until he was thirteen, when he moved to Lincoln, Illinois, to live with his mother and her husband, before the family eventually settled in Cleveland, Ohio. It was in Lincoln, Illinois, that Hughes began writing poetry. Following graduation, he spent a year in Mexico and a year at Columbia University. During these years, he held odd jobs as an assistant cook, launderer, and a busboy, and travelled to Africa and Europe working as a seaman. In November 1924, he moved to Washington, D.C. Hughes's first book of poetry, *The Weary Blues*, was published by Alfred A. Knopf in 1926. He finished his college education at Lincoln University in Pennsylvania three years later. In 1930 his first novel, *Not Without Laughter,* won the Harmon gold medal for literature.

Hughes, who claimed Paul Lawrence Dunbar, Carl Sandburg, and Walt Whitman as his primary influences, is particularly known for his insightful, colorful portrayals of black life in America from the twenties through the sixties. He wrote novels, short stories and plays, as well as poetry, and is also known for his engagement with the world of jazz and the influence it had on his writing, as in "Montage of a Dream Deferred." His life and work were enormously important in shaping the artistic contributions of the Harlem Renaissance of the 1920s. Unlike other notable black poets of the period—Claude McKay, Jean Toomer, and Countee Cullen—Hughes refused to differentiate between his personal experience and the common experience of black America. He wanted to tell the stories of his people in ways that reflected their actual culture, including both their suffering and their love of music, laughter, and language itself.

Langston Hughes died of complications from prostate cancer in May 22, 1967, in New York. In his memory, his residence at 20 East 127th Street in Harlem, New York City, has been given landmark status by the New York City Preservation Commission, and East 127th Street has been renamed "Langston Hughes Place."

[From the Academy of American Poets.org]

Dr. MAYA ANGELOU—GLOBAL RENAISSANCE WOMAN—Dr. Maya Angelou is one of the most renowned and influential voices of our time. Hailed as a global renaissance woman, Dr. Angelou is a celebrated poet, memoirist, novelist, educator, dramatist, producer, actress, historian, filmmaker, and civil rights activist. Born on April 4th, 1928, in St. Louis, Missouri, Dr. Angelou was raised in St. Louis and Stamps, Arkansas. In Stamps, Dr. Angelou experienced the brutality of racial discrimination, but she also absorbed the unshakable faith and values of traditional African-American family, community, and culture. As a teenager, Dr. Angelou's love for the arts won her a scholarship to study dance and drama at San Francisco's Labor School. In 1954 and 1955, Dr. Angelou toured Europe with a production of the opera *Porgy and Bess*. She studied modern dance with Martha Graham, danced with Alvin Ailey on television variety shows and, in 1957, recorded her first album, *Calypso Lady*. In 1958, she moved to New York, where she joined the Harlem Writers Guild, acted in the historic Off-Broadway production of Jean Genet's *The Blacks* and wrote and performed *Cabaret for Freedom*. In 1960, Dr. Angelou moved to Cairo, Egypt where she served as editor of the English language weekly *The Arab Observer*. The next year, she moved to Ghana where she taught at the University of Ghana's School of Music and Drama, worked as feature editor for *The African Review* and wrote for *The Ghanaian Times*. During her years abroad, Dr. Angelou read and studied voraciously, mastering French, Spanish, Italian, Arabic and the West African language Fanti. While in Ghana, she met with Malcolm X and, in 1964, returned to America to help him build his new Organization of African American Unity.

[Dr. Maya Angelou Official Web Site]

Carter G. Woodson

During the dawning decades of the twentieth century, it was commonly presumed that black people had little history besides the subjugation of slavery. Today, it is clear that blacks have significantly impacted the development of the social, political, and economic structures of the United States and the world. Credit for the evolving awareness of the true place of blacks in history can, in large part, be bestowed on one man, Carter G. Woodson. And, his brainchild the Association for the Study of African American Life and History, Inc. is continuing Woodson's tradition of disseminating information about black life, history and culture to the global community.

Known as the "Father of Black History," Woodson (1875–1950) was the son of former slaves, and understood how important gaining a proper education is when striving to secure and make the most out of one's divine right of freedom. Although he did not begin his formal education until he was 20 years old, his dedication to study enabled him to earn a high school diploma in West Virginia and bachelor and master's degrees from the University of Chicago in just a few years. In 1912, Woodson became the second African American to earn a Ph.D. from Harvard University (the first was W. E. B. DuBois). Applying the insights he gained during his academic matriculation, Dr. Woodson began teaching black students in the District of Columbia's public schools and at Howard University. Recognizing the dearth of information on the accomplishments of blacks in 1915, Dr. Woodson founded the Association for the Study of Negro Life and History, now called the Association for the Study of African American Life and History (ASALH). In 1926, Dr. Woodson initiated the celebration of Negro History Week, which corresponded with the birthdays of Frederick Douglass and Abraham Lincoln. In 1976, this celebration was expanded to include the entire month of February, and today Black History Month garners support throughout the country as people of all ethnic and social backgrounds discuss the black experience. ASALH views the promotion of Black History Month as one of the most important components of advancing Dr. Woodson's legacy.

[The ASALH web site]

Granville T. Woods.

OHIO HISTORICAL SOCIETY

Granville T. Woods

Granville T. Woods was an African-American inventor and was born on April 23, 1856, in Columbus, Ohio. He left school when he was ten years old and went to work to help support his family. Woods became an apprentice to a machinist. He learned blacksmithing and how to invent and repair machines. Woods continued his education by attending night school.

In 1872, Woods became a fireman on the Danville and Southern Railroad in Missouri. He was later promoted to engineer. After only two years with the railroad, Woods moved to Springfield, Illinois, where he accepted a position with a steel mill. By 1878, he had become an engineer on the Ironsides, a British steamship. Within two years, he had become the ship's chief engineer.

In all of the positions that he held, Woods experienced discrimination because of his race. Unhappy with his inability to obtain higher positions, Woods moved to Cincinnati, Ohio, where he established his own machine shop in 1880. The shop eventually became the Woods Electrical Company. Woods devoted his energies to developing an improved steam boiler in 1884. He also invented the first electric railway that was powered with electric lines from above the train. Previously the lines had run along the tracks and been quite dangerous to pedestrians. In addition to these inventions, Woods also created the first telegraph service that allowed messages to be sent from moving trains. This invention dramatically improved railroad safety. Woods also invented several improvements to the airbrakes used on locomotives and other large machines.

Woods sold his inventions to a number of companies, including the American Bell Telephone Company and the General Electric Company. By the time of his death on July 30, 1910, Woods had received more than sixty patents.

[Wikipedia.org]

Jack Roosevelt "Jackie" Robinson (January 31, 1919—October 24, 1972) was the first black Major League Baseball (MLB) player of the modern era. Robinson broke the baseball color line when he debuted with the Brooklyn Dodgers in 1947. As the first black man to play in the major leagues since the 1880s, he was instrumental in bringing an end to racial segregation in professional baseball, which had relegated black players to the Negro leagues for six decades. The example of his character and unquestionable talent challenged the traditional basis of segregation, which then marked many other aspects of American life, and contributed significantly to the Civil Rights Movement.

In addition to his cultural impact, Robinson had an exceptional baseball career. Over ten seasons, he played in six World Series and contributed to the Dodgers' 1955 World Championship. He was selected for six consecutive All-Star Games from 1949 to 1954, was the recipient of the inaugural MLB Rookie of the Year Award in 1947, and won the National League Most Valuable Player Award in 1949—the first black player so honored. Robinson was inducted into the Baseball Hall of Fame in 1962. In 1997, Major League Baseball retired his uniform number, 42, across all major league teams.

Robinson was also known for his pursuits outside the baseball diamond. He was the first black television analyst in Major League Baseball, and the first black vice-president of a major American corporation. In the 1960s, he helped establish the Freedom National Bank, an African-American-owned financial institution based in Harlem, New York. In recognition of his achievements on and off the field, Robinson was posthumously awarded the Presidential Medal of Freedom and the Congressional Gold Medal.

[Wikipedia.org]

U.S. NATIONAL ARCHIVES & RECORDS ADMINISTRATION

The Emancipation Proclamation
January 1, 1863
A Transcription
By the President of the United States of America:

A Proclamation.

Whereas, on the twenty-second day of September, in the year of our Lord one thousand eight hundred and sixty-two, a proclamation was issued by the President of the United States, containing, among other things, the following, to wit:

"That on the first day of January, in the year of our Lord one thousand eight hundred and sixty-three, all persons held as slaves within any State or designated part of a State, the people whereof shall then be in rebellion against the United States, shall be then, thenceforward, and forever free; and the Executive Government of the United States, including the military and naval authority thereof, will recognize and maintain the freedom of such persons, and will do no act or acts to repress such persons, or any of them, in any efforts they may make for their actual freedom.

"That the Executive will, on the first day of January aforesaid, by proclamation, designate the States and parts of States, if any, in which the people thereof, respectively, shall then be in rebellion against the United States; and the fact that any State, or the people thereof, shall on that day be, in good faith, represented in the Congress of the United States by members chosen thereto at elections wherein a majority of the qualified voters of such State shall have participated, shall, in the absence of strong countervailing testimony, be deemed conclusive evidence that such State, and the people thereof, are not then in rebellion against the United States."

Now, therefore I, Abraham Lincoln, President of the United States, by virtue of the power in me vested as Commander-in-Chief, of the Army and Navy of the United States in time of actual armed rebellion against the authority and government of the United States, and as a fit and necessary war measure for suppressing said rebellion, do, on this first day of January, in the year of our Lord one thousand eight hundred and sixty-three, and in accordance with my purpose so to do publicly proclaimed for the full period of one hundred days, from the day first above mentioned, order and designate as the States and parts of States wherein the people thereof respectively, are this day in rebellion against the United States, the following, to wit:

Arkansas, Texas, Louisiana, (except the Parishes of St. Bernard, Plaquemines, Jefferson, St. John, St. Charles, St. James Ascension, Assumption, Terrebonne, Lafourche, St. Mary, St. Martin, and Orleans, including the City of New Orleans) Mississippi, Alabama, Florida, Georgia, South Carolina, North Carolina, and Virginia, (except the forty-eight counties designated as West Virginia, and also the counties of Berkley, Accomac, Northampton, Elizabeth City, York, Princess Ann, and Norfolk, including the cities of Norfolk and Portsmouth[)], and which excepted parts, are for the present, left precisely as if this proclamation were not issued.

And by virtue of the power, and for the purpose aforesaid, I do order and declare that all persons held as slaves within said designated States, and parts of States, are, and henceforward shall be free; and that the Executive government of the United States, including the military and naval authorities thereof, will recognize and maintain the freedom of said persons.

And I hereby enjoin upon the people so declared to be free to abstain from all violence, unless in necessary self-defense; and I recommend to them that, in all cases when allowed, they labor faithfully for reasonable wages.

And I further declare and make known, that such persons of suitable condition, will be received into the armed service of the United States to garrison forts, positions, stations, and other places, and to man vessels of all sorts in said service.

And upon this act, sincerely believed to be an act of justice, warranted by the Constitution, upon military necessity, I invoke the considerate judgment of mankind, and the gracious favor of Almighty God.

In witness whereof, I have hereunto set my hand and caused the seal of the United States to be affixed.

Done at the City of Washington, this first day of January, in the year of our Lord one thousand eight hundred and sixty three, and of the Independence of the United States of America the eighty-seventh.

By the President: ABRAHAM LINCOLN
WILLIAM H. SEWARD, Secretary of State.

Marcus Mosiah Garvey, Jr., (17 August 1887—10 June 1940) was a publisher, journalist, entrepreneur, Black Nationalist, Pan-Africanist, and orator. Marcus Garvey was founder of the Universal Negro Improvement Association and African Communities League (UNIA-ACL). Prior to the twentieth century, leaders such as Prince Hall, Martin Delany, Edward Wilmot Blyden, and Henry Highland Garnet advocated the involvement of the African diaspora in African affairs. Garvey was unique in advancing a Pan-African philosophy to inspire a global mass movement focusing on Africa known as Garveyism Promoted by the UNIA as a movement of *African Redemption*, Garveyism would eventually inspire others, ranging from the Nation of Islam, to the Rastafari movement (which proclaims Garvey as a prophet). The intention of the movement was for those of African ancestry to "redeem" Africa. His essential ideas about Africa were stated in an editorial in the *Negro World* titled "African Fundamentalism" where he wrote: Our union must know no clime, boundary, or nationality…let us hold together under all climes and in every country

As a young man of fourteen, Garvey left school and worked as a printer's apprentice. He participated in Jamaica's earliest nationalist organizations, traveled throughout Central America, and spent time in London, England, where he worked with the Sudanese-Egyptian nationalist Duse Mohamed Ali. In 1916 Garvey was invited by Booker T. Washington to come to the United States in the hopes of establishing an industrial training school, but arrived just after Washington died. In March 1916, shortly after landing in America, Garvey embarked upon an extended period of travel. When he finally settled down, he organized a chapter of the Universal Negro Improvement Association and African Communities League. The UNIA & ACL had been formed in Jamaica in 1914. Its motto was "One God, One Aim, One Destiny," and pledged itself to the redemption of Africa and the uplift of Black people everywhere. It aimed at race pride, self-reliance and economic independence.

[Africawithin.com; Wikipedia.org]

CHAPTER 5

THE EDUCATION OF BOOKER

(THE LIFE AND TIME OF DR. MARTIN LUTHER KING, JR)

A PLAY

by Rita G. Fields
Copyright 1995

CAST OF CHARACTERS:

BOOKER: father

JANIE : mother

3 people at door

JODY : daughter

Daddy King

MARTIN

Narrators -23 Children

Teacher

Three White Men

Shoe Salesman

SCENE I

(SCENE OPENS WITH BOOKER T. AT HOME READING A NEWSPAPER. HIS WIFE, JANIE, IS SETING THE DINNER TABLE, WHEN THERE IS A KNOCK AT TIIE DOOR.)

JANIE: Booker honey, will you get the door?

(THE KNOCKS ARE HARDER. THERE ARE THREE PEOPLE AT THE DOOR WHEN HE OPENS IT)

1ST PERSON: Good evening sir, how are you this evening?

BOOKER: What you beggin' for??!

2ND PERSON: Excuse us! We are not beggars! We represent our Tenants Association's committee on Aid to the famine victims of Africa.

3RD PERSON: We're taking donations from concerned members of our community who want to help the many unfortunate brothers and sisters and children who are starving in Africa.

BOOKER: So, you're taking donations. That's the key word—TAKING- You're probably taking the money somewhere, and it won't be to Africa! I'm starving myself, right now, and y'all are keeping me from my dinner. I can't be worrying about Africa. And my brothers and sisters live right here! !

(SLAMS THE DOOR)

1ST PERSON: How insensitive!

2ND PERSON: How ignorant!

3RD PERSON: I hope that brother is going to wake up one day!

JANIE: Booker, come to the table. Dinner is ready. Who was that at the door Booker?

BOOKER: Some people begging for some folks in Africa,

JANIE: I hope you gave them a donation. It's the least we can do.

BOOKER: I didn't give them a penny.

JANIE (VERY UPSET): Why, Booker!!? Just why don't you care?

BOOKER: I don't care! I work hard every day and I put food on this table, and I take care of my family. I don't bother nobody and I'm tired of people bothering me.—Give to this, give to that— They need to help themselves.

JANIE: Everybody needs a little help every now and then Booker.

Daughter, JODY, walks in: Hi Ma and dad. What's up? I'm hungry.

BOOKER: What's up? You're late for dinner. Where you been all evening Jody?

JODY: I've been registering voters. It's amazing how many unregistered voters we have on our block alone.

JANIE: Well, you better start right in your own home and register your father.

JODY: Daddy, I know you're a registered voter! I can't believe it! You know how black people, many of them have died so that you could be given the right to vote.! Daddy, that's what the 60's was all about!

BOOKER: I am a registered voter, but I don't vote. I don't know when I voted last. Nobody is missing my vote and my vote won't change one thing. All that struggling, going to jail in the 60's changed some things, but not everything. So don't tell me about voting. My vote is just a needle in the haystack.—Pass me those biscuits!

JODY: Well, we need your vote daddy, believe it or not because we need every vote we can get to vote Mayor Edwards out of office. I think Percy Sullivan would make a more sensitive and fair mayor.

JANIE: I agree. I've been helping out with the campaign.

BOOKER: Y'all are wasting your time. No way, a black man's gonna be mayor of this city.

JODY: Don't say that! Black men and women are mayors of many large cities. There's Unita Blackwall, a woman, who was mayor of Mayersville, Mississippi, and Mayor Gibson of Newark, New Jersey, and what about Harold Washington, Mayor of Chicago?

JANIE: Don't forget Tom Bradley of Los Angeles, California, and David Dinkins, first African-American Mayor of New York City.

BOOKER: Well, that may be so, but I still say not in this city! Can't I express my opinion around here? I do have that right, don't I?

JANIE: Yes you do, and you do still have the right to vote. All we are trying to say is use it. It's your responsibility.

JODY: Dad, courageous men and women have lived their life in struggle so that millions after them could live in pride. The struggle to achieve equality, the right to vote came through civil action. We owe it to them not to abuse or not use those rights. Every time I ride the bus and sit where I please, I'm reminded of their struggle. When I walk into my college classroom I'm reminded of their struggle. And when I sit down to eat at any restaurant I choose, I am reminded of that struggle. I never want to forget and I want to do my share so those after me will enjoy the freedoms that I enjoy now. I think that's your problem, dad! You have forgotten about the struggles and the lives that were lost for Civil Rights. You need to be reminded! Excuse me!—I have some struggling to do! (SHE LEAVES THE TABLE)

BOOKER: I don't see why she has to get so emotional about the whole thing.

JANIE: (shaking her head): Listen. I'm going over to the church tonight. We're trying to organize a peaceful demonstration protesting the injustices of apartheid in South Africa. Why don't you come along? We need you.

BOOKER: South Africa is thousands of miles away. We can't help those folks overthere.

JANIE: A famous man—Martin Luther King, Jr.—once said, "We are tied together in one bond of common mutuality, and what affects some of us directly, affects all of us indirectly." That reminds me (she gets a book), Read this. It will help you to start caring again. Here. It's called: MARTIN LUTHER KING, JR.

His sister, Christine King Farris, wrote it.

BOOKER: I was planning on watching some television in my nice easy chair.

(WIFE EXITS. BOOKER SITS, CONTINUALLY SWITCHING CHANNELS THEN SAYS:)

I might as well turn it off, nothing's on. (HE PICKS UP BOOK AND BEGINS READING.)

SCENE II CHURCH

(*MUSIC PLAYING; (GOSPEL,) PEOPLE SINGING AND CLAPPING*)

NARRATOR 1:The heart of the Atlanta ghetto was centered in the churches. Ebenezer Baptist Church was Martin's family's church. His grandfather served as Pastor there for 37 years. Martin was two when his grandfather died But the church remained in the family, with Martin's father taking over as Pastor. All the time that Martin was growing up, the church was his second home. He heard his father preach a new way of life to his neighbors. The fiery young pastor begged his people to hold their heads up high and not to take abuse from anyone; but always to walk humbly with their God.

DADDY KING: Walk: proud hold your heads up high. Do not take abuse from anyone; but always—always walk humbly with your God!

PEOPLE IN CHURCH: Amen! (music; curtain closes)

NARRATOR 2: Martin Luther King's thirst for knowledge began early. His mother was a school teacher and she recognized that her son was an exceptionally bright child. So, even though he was only five (5) years old, she decided to enroll him in the first grade, hoping that he could pass as a six year old. Everything was going along fine until one day he let his age slip out.

SCENE III (AT SCHOOL)

MARTIN: (comes out with a piece of cake; his friends surround him) Who wants a piece of cake?

CHILDREN: I'll take a piece, me too, me too.

MARTIN: Yep, yesterday was my birthday, (at this time teacher comes out) and I got a lot of presents and I had a big birthday cake with 5 big candles.

TEACHER: Five big candles? Why Martin, you are only 5 years old. You are too young to be here. Sorry but you'll have to come with me to call your parents. You have to go home!

NARRATOR 3: Martin came back to school the following year. But he hadn't been in school long before he was skipped.

NARRATOR 4: It wasn't long after Martin started school that he began to read signs in his neighborhood and around the city. One of the first things he learned to read was signs like this: (sign carrier comes out holding sign saying…)

"FOR WHITES ONLY.' Or when he rode the bus or street cars, signs like this: "COLORED SIT IN THE BACK"; "COLORED ENTER AND EXIT BY BACK DOOR". Martin soon learned that these signs were a part of life for the segregated south. Segregation was a system that kept blacks and whites separated. There were segregated schools, restaurants, theatres; segregated housing, even separate water fountains and bathrooms. There were laws that were very unfair to black people—these unfair laws were called JIM CROW LAWS. It was soon time for Martin to get a taste of the Jim Crow, segregated, South.

SCENE IV- (DADDY KING AND YOUNG MARTIN)

DADDY KING: C'mon Martin, get in the car. Lets go downtown. (begin driving)

POLICE: Stop the car! Lets see your license boy!

DADDY KING: (Reaches for license, but before he handed it to the policeman he says:) "He's a boy. I'm a man!

DADDY KING: C'mon Martin let's get you some shoes. (They sit down in shoe store)

SHOE SALESMAN: (Comes with boxes of shoes) I'll be glad to serve you, if you'd sit in those seats at the back of the store.

DADDY KING: Nothing wrong with these seats, thank you.

SALESMAN: But we don't serve colored people in front of the store.

DADDY KING: Well if you don't serve colored people in front of the store, you don't serve these colored at all! (Takes Martin by the hand and marches out)

NARRATOR 5: At the early age of fifteen, Martin was ready to enter college. He entered Morehouse College in Atlanta in 1944. Morehouse College was a great Black institution, 65 years old. Its founder was a black minister, the Rev. William Jefferson White, and it was supported by both black and white Baptists. Its students were all black. Morehouse was respected as a school that produced great men. Among them Martin's own father. Everyone felt certain that Martin would follow his father into the ministry. But Martin was not sure. Above everything else, he wanted to choose a career in which he could help his people in the best possible way.

(MEANWHILE, MARTIN IS AT A DESK LOOKING UNDECIDED. SIGN CARRIERS HOLD UP SIGNS THAT SAY: LAWYER?; DOCTOR?; MINISTER?)

NARRATOR 6: In the end, it was an essay that helped Martin make up his mind. It was an essay entitled "Civil Disobedience" by Henry David Thoreau. Thoreau felt that the poll tax law which required him to pay for the right to vote was unjust. So he did not pay the tax and was arrested and jailed. Martin began to see that Thoreau's techniques of civil disobedience might be used to help Black people to gain their rights. He felt the best way to get his ideas across to many Black people was to come before them as a man of God, a minister. A new kind of minister who would lead his people to freedom! Shortly after he entered the senior class at Morehouse, 18 year old Martin was ordained as a minister and elected assistant pastor of Ebenezer Baptist Church. It was a jubilant day for everyone, particularly Martin's father.

SCENE V (CHURCH)

MARTIN: (PREACHING HIS FIRST SERMON) If you will protest courageously, and yet with dignity and Christian love, when the history books are written in future generations, the historians will have to pause and say, 'There lived a great people, a black people, who injected new meaning and dignity into the veins of civilization.' This is our challenge and our overwhelming responsibility.

NARRATOR 8: After graduating from Morehouse in 1948, Martin entered Crozer Theological Seminary in Chester, Pennsylvania. Going to Crozer was different from Morehouse. First of all Crozer was in the North. Second of all, there were 100 white students and only 6 black students. One of the white students, from North Carolina, did not like black people.

SCENE VI

(CROZER THEOLOGICAL SEMINARY, DORM ROOM)

(A GROUP OF WHITE MEN LAUGHING)

WHITE MAN: We sure tore up that room.

WHITE MAN 2: It'll take him forever to clean up that mess. (THEY AIL START LAUGHING)

WHITE MAN FROM NORTH CAROLINA: Why don't y'all come to my room for a little while?

(CURTAINS OPEN, HIS ROOM IS A MESS)

WHITE MAN: Holly Cow!!!

WHITE MAN 2: What a wreck!!!

WHITE MAN FROM N.C.: I bet you one of those no good darkies did this. I'm gonna kill him! It was that Martin Luther King! C'mon y'all !

(THEY WALK TO CENTER STAGE)

WHITE MAN FROM N.C. : Hey you! You no good darkie. I know it was you who messed up my room and you better get your tail in there and clean it up!

MARTIN: I don't know what you're talking about. I have been in the library all morning. You're wrong if you think its me. You can even ask the librarian. she saw me.

WHITE MAN: You liar! I ought to put a bullet in your head! (Pulls out a gun)

NARRATOR 9: This incident was brought before the student board and faculty. Martin refused to press charges. Finally the white student publicly apologized and admitted that he was wrong. He and Martin became very good friends at Crozier. Martin later became acquainted with the teachings of Mahatma Gandhi. Who, like Thoreau freed his people from British oppressors. He allowed his people to break laws that seemed unjust. And urged his followers not to strike back at the police who sometimes beat them. Thoreau also taught love for the oppressor, not hate.

SCENE VII

(MARTIN HOLDING TWO BOOKS, THOREAU AND GHANDI).

MARTIN: Why not combine the teachings and ideas of Jesus Christ, Thoreau, and Gandhi? Jesus said 'Love your enemies". Like Thoreau and Gandhi we could rebel against unjust laws, but do it peacefully. I know it could work here in America. How could I get it across, where, Lord? When? I know it won't be easy to bring these new ideas to black people. I must be patient and wait for the right moment.

NARRATOR 10: (MARTIN DRESSED IN GRADUATION ROBE, ACCEPTING DIPLOMA) Martin graduated from Crozer at twenty-two years of age. He was the valedictorian of his class—the top of his class. He received many honors, among them was $1200 dollars to be applied to two years at a college of his choice. Martin chose Boston University where he received the highest degree in education—a doctorate. (ENTER CORETTA, SHE TAKES MARTIN'S ARM) In Boston he met the lovely Coretta Scott, who was studying voice and music at the New England Conservatory. She and Martin were married on June 18, 1953. The ceremony was performed by Martin's father in the garden of Coretta's home. By the time the newlyweds had completed their year of school, they were faced with a serious decision.

SCENE VIII

(CORETTA AND MARTIN SITTING AT TABLE)

MARTIN: Coretta, I don't know what to do. I've been offered three (3) jobs from three different colleges and three churches. Two of them right here in the north want me as their pastor.

CORETTA: Where is the third church Martin?

MARTIN: It's in the South, in Montgomery, Alabama.

CORETTA: I don't know if I want to live in the South again. There is a lot of prejudice. There is a lot of prejudice right here in the North, but I think we could lead an easier life here.

MARTIN: I know what you mean. The South treats Black folk so mean. All of those Jim Crow laws. I don't know if I could take that treatment after living here in the North.

CORETTA: But I do miss my family and friends.

MARTIN: With all the South's faults, it's still home.

NARRATOR 11: Martin accepted the pastorate of Dexter Avenue Baptist Church in Montgomery, Alabama. Together, the young couple headed back to the South where they were both born, hoping to help shape a brighter future for their people. Things had not changed much when Dr. King arrived in Montgomery. Black people still had to take their seats in the back of the bus. Dr. King started speaking out plainly against such injustices in his Sunday Sermon. He also started talking to other ministers and to Black leaders in the community about Gandhi and non-violence.

SCENE IX

(AT CHURCH WI1H GROUP OF MINISTERS)

MARTIN: What would happen if Black people stopped riding the buses as a protest? Surely the bus company would have to change it's rules?

MINISTER: Martin, it might work someday, but not now, perhaps in the future.

NARRATOR 12: Then one day, after Dr. King had been in Montgomery over a year and there was still only talk among Black people about doing something to help themselves, a middle aged woman named Rosa Parks did something.

SCENE X (BUS SCENE)

(CURTAINS OPEN, BUS IS SHOWN WITH PASSENGERS. ROSA PARKS GETS ON, PAYS HER FARE AND TAKES SEAT BEHIND A SIGN READING: "RESERVED FOR WHITE". THREE OTHER BLACK PEOPLE ALSO SIT NEAR HER IN THE WHITE SECTION. AS THE BUS STOPS, WHITE PEOPLE GET ON AND THE OTHER BLACK PEOPLE GIVE UP THEIR SEATS.) BUS DRNER: O.K. lady, stand up and let someone sit down. (ROSA REMAINS SEATED) BUS DRIVER: Did you hear me? Get up out of that seat right now, or I'm gonna get the police.

ROSA: Well, you will have to get the police. MY feet are tired and I paid the same fare as they did. Why should I stand?

BUS DRIVER: (SIGNALS FOR POLICE) Officer, we have trouble here.

OFFICERS: What's the problem?

BUS DRIVER: She won't get up and let the white passenger sit down. I told her twice!

OFFICERS: You are breaking the law. You're under arrest. Lets go!

(THEY GRAB HER BY THE ARM TO TAKE HER TO JAIL.)

NARRATOR 13: That night a meeting of Black leaders was held in Dr. King's church. The ministers who were present agreed to speak to their congregations on Sunday about the tremendous importance of their refusing to ride the busses. The group also planned to print and distribute seven thousand leaflets notifying the Black community of the bus boycott. When Monday morning finally came, Martin and his wife were up at 5:30 a.m. to see how effective the boycott was.

(SHOW EMPTY BUS; BLACK PEOPLE WAKING BY)

They watched as bus, after bus, rode by empty, or with white passengers only. That afternoon, at a meeting of boycott leaders, Dr. King was unanimously elected president of a newly formed organization, The Montgomery Improvement Association. At a mass meeting that night, the Holt Street Church was overflowing with people. Before Dr. King rose to speak, the huge crowd lifted its voice in the opening hymn, "Onward Christian Soldier."

SCENE XI

NARRATOR 14: For 381 days black people did not ride the buses in Montgomery. People walked or rode mules or drove horse and wagon rigs. Black owned taxi cab services agreed to let passengers ride at bus fare rates. Soon it was obvious to the owners of the bus company and to the white community that the black people were not going to ride the buses unless their terms were met

SCENE XII

(BUS OWNERS AND BLACKS AT MEETING)

BUS OWNERS: What is it that you black people want from us?

BLACK PERSON #1: We want courteous treatment from drivers.

B.P. #2: We want to be able to sit and enter the bus wherever we want.

B.P. #3: We want you to hire black bus drivers. (HANDS PAPER WITH TERMS TO BUS OWNERS)

BUS OWNERS: Is that so? (They begin laughing) Sorry, we can't meet those terms.

(RIPS UP PAPERS WITH TERMS.)

NARRATOR 15: The bus company and the city officials would not agree to the black people's terms. The police began arresting black people on trumped-up charges.For instance, black people waiting to be picked up by a car pool were threatened with arrest as hitch-hikers.

(SHOW BLACK PEOPLE WAITING FOR RIDE BEING HARRASSED)

Even Dr. King was arrested and put in jail. But he was released in no time. And then, while some people used more violent methods to force black people to end the boycott, a bomb was tossed on Dr. King's porch.

(MARTIN, WIFE AND BABY RUN FROM BEHIND CURTAIN. CORETTA UPSET AND MARTIN COMFORTING HER.)

Luckily his wife and baby were not hurt.

SCENE XIII (KING BEFORE JUDGE)

NARRATOR 16: After three months a Montgomery Grand Jury met and said the boycott was illegal. They arrested one hundred boycotters and their leaders. Dr. King was also arrested. After a four day trial, Dr. King was found guilty. JUDGE: You, Dr. Martin Luther King, are found guilty of violating our state's anti-boycott laws. I sentence you to pay a fine of $500 dollars or to serve 386 days at hard labor in the county jail.

(DR. KING BEING LED AWAY BY GUARDS)

NARRATOR 16: Quickly, a Notice of Appeal was filed and Dr. King was released. In November, lawyers for the city of Montgomery took the case to the United States Supreme Court, the highest court in the land. The Supreme Court ruled that Alabama's bus segregation laws were unconstitutional. That means the laws were unfair and against the laws of the United States.

After 381 days of walking for freedom, Montgomery's 50,000 black citizens, with Dr. Martin Luther King, Jr. as their leader, won out against injustice! Black people had the right to sit anywhere in a bus that they pleased

SCENE XIV

(BLACKS, ARM IN ARM, ENTER RESTAURANT; GO TO TABLE AND SIT DOWN)

BLACK PERSON: I'd like some service here, please.

WAITRESS: We don't serve black people in here. Get out before I call the police!

BLACK PERSON: I am hungry. I'd like service.

WAITRESS: OK! You asked for it!

POLICE: Get up! You're under arrest. No Blacks are allowed in here!

(POLICE DRAG THE PROTESTORS AWAY)

NARRATOR 17: The Clergy of all faiths joined the movement. White ministers were jailed for freedom riding. Freedom riding meant that groups of white people and black people from all over the country boarded buses in the South and sat together in the white sections. Jewish Rabbis fasted and prayed in the jails of the South. A Catholic Bishop insisted that the white schools in his diocese admit black people.

NARRATOR 18: The surge toward freedom was answered by the burning of four black churches in Georgia. A white mailman walking the roads as a lone freedom marcher was murdered in Alabama. Medger Evers, a black leader, was shot to death. Many others were also killed. One of the worst attacks was during demonstrations in Birmingham. Dr. King and 2500 people were attacked by fire hoses being turned on them full force, and by attack dogs. They and Dr. King, were arrested. Dr. King was held in solitary confinement. His wife, Coretta, was worried because she was unable to hear from him. She received a telephone call from President John F. Kennedy assuring her that her husband was safe.

NARRATOR 19: On August 28, 1963, the March on Washington was held. Young and old, black and white, Gentile and Jew; housewives, sharecroppers, all gathered on the slope of the Washington Monument. Shoulder to shoulder they marched to the Lincoln Memorial. These people marched to Washington to call attention to segregation and unfair laws against black people. They marched for decent housing, equal pay, equal job opportunities, and equal voting rights. No violence broke out as expected in that crowd of over 250,000 people. The highlight of the day came when Dr. King arose to speak.

SCENE XV (DR. KING AT PODIUM)

DR. KING: (MAKES FAMOUS SPEECH)….I say to you today my friends, even though we face the difficulties of today and tomorrow, I still have a dream. It is dream deeply rooted in the American dream. I have a dream that one day this nation will rise up and live up to it's creed: "We hold these truths to be self-evident, that all men are created equal." I have a dream that one day on the red hills of Georgia, the sons of former slaves, and the sons of former slave owners, will be able to sit down together at the table of brotherhood. I have a dream that one day, even the state of Mississippi, a state sweltering with the heat of injustice, sweltering with the heat of oppression, will be transformed into an oasis of freedom and justice. I have a dream that my four little children will one day live in a nation where they will not be judged by the color of their skin—but by the content of their character. I have a dream today!

I have a dream that one day down in Alabama, with its vicious racists, with its Governor…having his lips dripping with the words of interposition* and nullification*.

One day right down there in Alabama, little black boys and little black girls will be able to join hands with little white boys and little white girls as sisters and brothers.

I have a dream today!

I have a dream that one day every valley shall be exalted, every hill and mountain shall be made low, the rough places made plain, the crooked places made straight; And the glory of the Lord shall be revealed, and all flesh shall see it together.

This is our hope, this is the faith that I go back to the South with.

With this faith, we will be able to hew out of the mountain of despair a stone of hope.

With this faith, we will be able to transform the jangling* discords" of our nation into a beautiful symphony of brotherhood.

With this faith, we will be able to work together, pray together, struggle together, go to jail together, stand up for freedom together; knowing that we will be free.

This will be the day when all of God's children will be able to sing with new meaning—"My country 'tis of thee, sweet land of liberty, of thee I sing. Land where my fathers died, land of the Pilgrims pride, from every mountain side, let freedom ring!"

If America is to become a great nation, this must become true.

So, let freedom ring from the prodigious hill tops of New Hampshire.

Let freedom ring from the mighty mountains of New York.

Let freedom ring from the heightening Alleghenies of Pennsylvania.

Let freedom ring from the snow-capped Rockies of Colorado.

Let freedom ring from the curvaceous slopes of California.

But not only that.

Let freedom ring from Stone Mountain of Georgia.

Let freedom ring from Look-Out Mountain of Tennessee.

Let freedom ring from every hill and molehill of Mississippi—FROM EVERY MOUNTAIN SIDE!

Let freedom ring. And when this happens; When we let it ring from every state and every city, we will be able to speed up that day when all of God's children,

Black men and White men, Jews and Gentiles, Protestants and Catholics, will be able to join hands and sing in the words of the old Negro Spiritual:

"Free at last, free at last, thank God Almighty, we are free at last!"

NARRATOR 20: On October 14, 1964, Dr. King received the Nobel Peace Prize. The Peace Prize is one of the five Nobel Prizes which are given each year to worthy recipients.

At 35 years old, Dr. King was the youngest person ever to win the award; and the second black person to win it. The first black person who won the Nobel Peace prize was Dr.Ralph Bunche. The Nobel Prize was presented to Dr. King in Oslo, Norway on December 10, 1964 by Gunnar Jahn, the Chairman of the Nobel Peace Prize Committee.

SCENE XVI (DR. KING RECEIVING NOBEL PRIZE)

DR. JAHN: Today we present the Nobel Peace Prize to a champion of peace.

The first person in the Western world to have shown us that a struggle can be waged without violence;- Dr. Martin Luther King, Jr.!

DR. KING: I accept this award on behalf of the civil rights movement

NARRATOR 21: On April 3, 1968, Dr. King went to Memphis, Tennessee to help striking garbage workers. All day on April 4th, he met with his staff at the Lorrain Motel. Before going to dinner, Dr. King leaned over the balcony of his room and chatted with staff aids. Suddenly, a shot rang out!

(SHOW DR. KING WITH AIDS; AND DROPPING TO GROUND AFTER SHOTS)

(CURTAINS CLOSE)

NARRATOR 22: At 7:00 that evening, Dr. King died of a gunshot wound in the neck. The peaceful warrior was gone. The public was overwhelmed with grief Millions of people paid tribute to this man of non-violence. On his crypt, some very simple words were written. They are words from an old slave song that Dr. King often used to end his speeches. They probably would be his words now if he could speak them: "Free at last, Free at last, Thank God Almighty, I'm free at last.!"

SCENE XVII

(AT BOOKER'S HOME)

BOOKER: (Closes book) What a human being!

How dare I take things for granted??! !

(DAUGHTER ENTERS)

JODY: Talking to yourself, Daddy?

BOOKER: Oh no! I was just wondering…tomorrow is Saturday and I don't have to go to work. I was wondering, if you need any help with registering people to vote?

JANIE (Walks in): I'm home.

JODY: You mean, you want to help register people to vote? I know this can't be the same father I left sitting in this room earlier this evening.

(WIFE GOES OVER AND PICKS UP BOOK AND NODS HER HEAD AT BOOKER)

BOOKER: No. I'm not quite the same. I think you'll like this person a lot better.

(Looks at wife) Dear what time is that demonstration against apartheid tomorrow? We'd better get some rest if we're going.

(Wife and daughter look surprised) (They hug Booker)

(CURTAINS CLOSE)

NARRATOR 23: As you all know, President Ronald Reagan signed a bill on November 2,1983 establishing the third Monday in January as the Dr. Martin Luther King Holiday. Each year on Martin Luther King Day, let us all rededicate ourselves to the things he believed in. Dr. King made a positive impact on the character in our play, but in reality, he made an impact upon all Americans. His message was simple. Try to see each person as a brother or sister. Look for ways in which we are similar, not different. Commit yourself to world peace. Try not to make assumptions based on race. These are the presents we can give to Dr. King's memory on his birthday.

THE BEGINNING

CHAPTER 6

WAKUM

"THE TIME TRAVELER"

By Rita G. Fields

Copyright 1995

CAST OF CHARACTERS

TEACHER—MRS. JONES

NARRATOR

9 STUDENTS

BILL

GINA

BOBBY

JERRY

ROSA PARKS

MARTIN LUTHER KING

MALCOLM X

WAKUM

BUS DRIVER

POLICEMAN

WHITE MAN

AFRICAN DANCERS

GROUP OF EXTRAS

WAKUM—THE TIME TRAVELER
PLAY...by Rita Fields
ACT I

SCENE I

(Curtains Closed)

NARRATOR: As we all know, February is Black History Month. Have you been studying Black History in your class? Good! So has Mrs. Jones' class. This week they've learned many important facts about the Civil Rights Movement. Do you know anything about the Civil Rights Movement? Let's see if they know as much as you do. Oh, 'wait, there's Bill, a student from Mrs. Jones' class now. Let's ask him to tell us about the Civil Rights Movement.

(Bill is walking down the center aisle reading a book entitled Black History. He is approached as he reaches the stage)

NARRATOR: Excuse me. (Bill is enthralled with the book he's reading) Excuse Me! (Bill jumps, startled) I didn't mean to scare you, but my friends (points to audience) and I were wondering if you could tell us what the Civil Rights period was all about?

BILL: Wow! (pointing to audience) you sure do have a lot of friends! So, you want to know about the Civil Rights period. Well, (looking at his watch) I don't think Mrs. Jones will be angry if I'm late for a very good reason. What was the question?

NARRATOR: What was the Civil Rights Movement?

BILL: Oh! That's easy! The Civil Rights Movement was a time when Afro-Americans fought for their human and civil rights. Human rights are the rights of each human being to life, liberty, dignity and respect as a person without distinction of any kind. Civil Rights are those rights of a citizen which are guaranteed in the Constitution. I'd like to tell you more, but I'm really late! Hey, I have a great idea. I'll leave the door to our classroom open and you and your friends can listen in.

NARRATOR: Great idea, let's go. (motions to audience) (As Bill walks towards curtains they open)

Classroom: (Students are busy working and reading as Mrs. Jones walks around checking work. Bill enters classroom.)

BILL: Sorry I'm late. Should I leave the door open?

MRS. JONES: Yes you can leave it open. But why are you late Bill?

BILL: Am I late? I didn't realize it was so late, but on my way to school", (Mrs. Jones cuts in)

MRS. JONES: Never mind Bill. Take out last night's homework and let's go over the Black History questions. First question—What were some public schools like during the 1960's?

STUDENT # 1: Schools in some areas of our country were very different than our schools today. During that time black children and white children were not allowed to go to the same schools. Black people had their own schools and white people had their own schools. This separation was called segregation.

MRS. JONES: Very good! But today our schools are not segregated. How did things change?

STUDENT #2: In 1954, a case known as Brown vs. Board of Education, the Supreme Court ruled that racial segregation in the public schools was unconstitutional. Now black and white children would not have to go to separate schools. This was called integration.

MRS. JONES: Excellent! We must also remember that the law would not have changed if it weren't for many dedicated people who fought for a change. Remember, things can't change for the better unless people work together to make a change. On that note, I'll give you your next assignment. We have talked about many brave and interesting people who worked hard to make our country a fair and better place for us all. For homework, you are to do a report on one person who was a part of the Civil Rights Movement. Are there any questions?

STUDENT #3: Mrs. Jones, there are so many people who worked hard for Civil Rights. How do we choose just one?

MRS JONES: That's true. It'll be hard to choose one. But choose the one who inspired you the most. Think about the one you'd like to meet if you'd lived during that time. Let's pack up! Time to go home!

(CURTAINS CLOSE)

SCENE II

(THREE STUDENTS, GINA, BOBBY AND JERRY, COME ON STAGE CARRYING BOOKS
ON THEIR WAY HOME. STUDENTS ARE VERY ENTHUSIASTIC)

BOBBY: I already know who I'm doing my report on. **Dr. Martin Luther King Jr.**

GINA: I'm doing my report on a great black woman; no doubt about it. I'm doing my report on the
Mother of the Civil Rights Movement, **Rosa Parks.**

JERRY: I'll bet you nobody will do a report on my choice—**Malcolm X.**

GINA: Well, Mrs. Jones did say to do it on a person we'd like to meet if we lived during that time.
And I'd love to have been there giving Rosa my support and walking instead of riding the bus.

BOBBY: Wow! Wouldn't that be great if we could go back into time and see Dr. King give some
of his famous speeches? What about you Bookworm?

(He nudges Jerry who is now reading a book entitled Malcolm X)

JERRY: You people have some imaginations because there's no way we could go back to that time.

GINA: I have an idea! We may not be able to go back in time, but we can go to the library and get
started on our reports.

BOBBY: Good idea. Let's go.

**(Students proceed to library. On the way, smoke appears, and a man appears with the smoke
(WAKUM) Children grab each other. Terrified, they don't move)**

JERRY: Who on earth are you? What do you want from us?

WAKUM: Please don't be afraid. I am not here to hurt you. Allow me to introduce myself. My name is Wakum, the time traveler. I'm not in the habit of eaves dropping but I overheard a conversation you were having about going back into time.

Well, today is your lucky day! I am here to take you back (pointing to Gina) to the days when a brave woman started a movement because she was too tired to give up her seat—the Mother of the Civil Rights Movement—Rosa Parks. (Pointing to Bobby) Back to the time when Dr Martin Luther King Jr. won Civil Rigits for his people. (Pointing to Jerry) Back to the days when Malcolm X was giving direction to Black people. Back to the days when the word Negro became Black And, Black became beautiful!

JERRY: Man, you've got to be joking!

BOBBY: Yeah. You've been watching too much TV, You're bugging out!

GINA: Yeah. Too much Star Trek!

WAKUM: **Joking? Too much TV? Star Trek?! Does this look like I'm a fake?**

(He points his hands as if to say "abra cadabra"; and smoke appears.)

GINA: (GRABBING THE TWO BOYS AND PULLING THEM TO THE SIDE) Excuse us Wakum, we'll get back to you in a minute! C'mon guys, I really think he is a Time Traveler. This would be great. We'd get to see our heroes. C'mon, let's go!

BOBBY: You're right. He convinced me with all that smoke—I'm down!

JERRY: (Shakes his head and leads them all over to Wakum) O.K. Mr. Time Traveler!?

WAKUM: Please, just call me Wakum.

JERRY: O.K. Wakum. Where do we go first?

WAKUM: Didn't I hear you mention Rosa Parks (Pointing to Gina)? Let's go back to the beginning of the Civil Rights Movement.

(TIME TRAVELNG MUSIC PLAYS AS THEY WALK AROUND AUDITORIUM.THEY COME DOWN CENTER AISLE. AS THEY APPROACH STAGE, SIGN CARRIER COMES OUT HOLDING SIGN THAT SAYS" DECEMBER. 1, 1955',)

ACT II

SCENE III

(CURTAINS OPEN, PEOPLE SEATED ON A BUS. BLACKS IN BACK WHITES IN FRONT)

BUS DRIVER: (Yells) Next stop Maple Street! *(Black student gets on bus, pays and goes to back of bus.)*

ROSA: *(GETS ON BUS AND SITS IN FRONT SEAT—WHITE SECTION)* WHITEMAN: *(WALKS ON BUS. STANDS OVER ROSA)*

BUS DRIVER: Don't you see that the man wants a seat? Get up and give him your seat!

ROSA: *(DOESN'T MOVE-She ignores him)*

BUS DRIVER: Don't you hear me talking to you?

ROSA: I have worked hard all day. I'm tired. My feet hurt. I paid the same fare as he did. Why should I have to move?

BUS DRIVER: You know it's the law. Coloreds in the back, whites in the front. Now get up or I'll call the police!

ROSA: Well, you just have to call the police, because I'm not moving.

BUS DRIVER: (Yells to police Officer) Officer! Officer!

POLICEMAN: What's going on here?

BUS DRIVER: This colored woman will not go to the back.

POLICEMAN: You are breaking the law. You're under arrest. *(HAND CUFFS HER)*

(CURTAIN CLOSES)

(CURTAINS CLOSED)

NARRATOR: The arrest of Ms. Rosa Parks was the last straw to the Negro community. Within 24 hours, the community and community leaders decided to call a bus boycott and keep some 17000 Negroes from riding the public buses.

JERRY: I forgot. What does boycott mean?

GINA: Boycott means to refuse to use or buy services.

BOBBY: Yeah. When they boycotted the bus company, they didn't ride the bus for 382 days—over a year!

GINA: Instead of buses, they used car pools, horses, and some even walked.

WAKUM: This boycott was organized by a 27 year old preacher. He became the leader of the Civil Rights Movement.

BOBBY: You're talking about Dr. Martin Luther King Jr.

WAKUM: Dr. King soon became known for his stirring speeches. Many of them were given in Atlanta, Georgia at the Ebenezer Baptist Church.

SCENE IV

(CHURCH: AS CURTAINS OPEN, CHOIR BEGINS SINGING GOSPEL SONG. AFTER SONG, DR. KING COMES TO PULPIT)

DR. KING: Brothers and sisters, today we celebrate a victory. The Supreme Court has ruled that segregated seating on buses is unconstitutional. Together, we must continue to work and fight the injustices of this system.

CONGREGATION: 'Amen"

CHOIR: (SINGS) "IF I COULD HELP SOMEBODY"

BOBBY: Where to next?

WAKUM: Now to a period where the word Negro was replaced with the word Black and the concept of black is beautiful prevailed. The slogan Black Power became popular during this period.

GINA: I've seen pictures from those times. Almost everyone had the same hairstyle.

WAKUM: You could see black men and women and children wearing a hairstyle called the Afro, along with beautiful African clothing. They were telling the world that they were Black and Proud.

(FASHION SHOW PERFORMED TO JAMES BROW'N'S SONG 'TM BLACK

AND I'M PROUD")

(Curtains close)

WAKUM: Yes. During those days, Black people exhibited strong ties with Africa. This was evident in their walk, their talk and their Dance.

(CURTAINS OPEN: AFRICAN DANCE IS PERFORMED)

JERRY: Wow! That was great!

W AKUM: The trip wouldn't be complete without Malcolm X. He was one of the most outstanding advocates of black power.

GINA: At first, Malcolm X disliked white people. He was angry at the way they treated black people.

WAKUM: Malcolm liked being among the people. He could always be found speaking to the everyday people; trying to instill a sense of hope and pride in them,

MALCOLM X: A-salaam A-laakem! My brothers and sisters! That means peace unto you in Arabic. My name is Malcolm X. Many people think that I did not want the black man and white man to live together. This was true at one time. But then I changed my mind after a religious pilgrimage to Mecca. I guess you could say that I just wanted my black brothers and sisters to hold their heads up high and be proud people. I wanted them to learn about their beautiful culture and respect themselves and command respect from others.

BOBBY: We should be proud. We have talented people in all walks of life.

GINA: Yes, we do; science, sports, math, literature, entertainment:

(Curtains open to class room scene. Students #4 thru 9 recite names of famous people in major fields)

STUDENT #4: SCIENCE: Benjamin Banneker, Garrett Morgan, Granville T. Woods, Robert F. Fleming Jr., John Standard,William P. Purvis.

STUDENT #5: MEDICINE: Dr. Charles Drew, and Dr. Daniel Hale Williams

STUDENT#6: SPORTS: Althea Gibson, Muhammad Ali, Jackie Robinson, Jesse Owens.

STUDENT#7: LITERATURE: Nikki Giovanni, Lorraine Hansberry, Carter G. Woodson, Richard 'Wright, Langston Hughes.

STUDENT #8: POLITICS: Jesse Jackson, Thurgood Marshall, Shirley Chisholm, Barbara Jordan, Ralph Bunche.

STUDENT #9: ENTERTAINMENT: Michael Jackson, Sammy Davis Jr., Bill Cosby, Diana Ross and the Supremes.

WAKUM: Be it tap, ballet or modem dance, Black people have been a leading force in the field of dance. One of the lead choreographers during the Civil Rights period was Alvin Ailey. One of his greatest works has become a classic around the world.

GINA: Do you mean "Revelations"?

WAKUM: Yes. One of Alvin Aileys' most creative works, "Revelations".

(REVELATIONS DANCE IS PERFORMED)

BOBBY: Wow! That was fantastic. But all this time traveling has made me hungry.

GINA: How can you think of food at a time like this?

WAKUM: Well, it's getting late. I think that's enough time traveling for one day.

Lets go back home.

(TIME TRAVELING MUSIC PLAYS)

WAKUM: I hope that you've learned something today.

JERRY: Learn something! This has been an experience of a life time.

GINA: I'm sure that I can speak for us all when I say that the Civil Rights Movement was a time of struggle for equality and dignity.

BOBBY: Through it all, Black people gained a sense of pride and awareness of the beauty and richness of our culture.

JERRY: And don't forget that despite the many obstacles, black people continued to achieve and contribute to this country.

WAKUM: Well, I can see that my job is done.

BOBBY: What happens now?

WAKUM: What happens now is that you must remember those who fought for the rights and freedoms that (points to audience) you and you enjoy now.

It's all up to you all to make the world a better place.

(WAKUM EXITS IN A CLOUD OF SMOKE)

GINA: It's up to us to make the world a better place. We've got to make a change…

Say, I've heard those words before.

(SONG, "MAN IN THE MIRROR" PLAYS)

THE END

copyright 1995

CHAPTER 7

HISTORICAL FIGURES MENTIONED IN THE PLAY

Rosa Louise McCauley Parks (February 4, 1913—October 24, 2005) was an African American civil rights activist, whom the U.S. Congress later called "the first lady of civil rights", and "the mother of the freedom movement".http://en.wikipedia.org/wiki/Rosa_Parks - cite_note-0

On December 1, 1955 in Montgomery, Alabama, Parks, age 42, refused to obey bus driver James Blake's order that she give up her seat to make room for a white passenger. Parks' action sparked the Montgomery Bus Boycott.

Parks' act of defiance became an important symbol of the modern Civil Rights Movement and Parks became an international icon of resistance to racial segregation. She organized and collaborated with civil rights leaders, including boycott leader Martin Luther King, Jr., helping to launch him to national prominence in the civil rights movement.

At the time of her action, Parks was secretary of the Montgomery chapter of the National Association for the Advancement of Colored People (NAACP) and had recently attended the Highlander Folk School, a Tennessee center for workers' rights and racial equality. Nonetheless, she took her action as a private citizen "tired of giving in". Although widely honored in later years for her action, she suffered for it, losing her job as a seamstress in a local department store. Eventually, she moved to Detroit, Michigan, where she found similar work. From 1965 to 1988 she served as secretary and receptionist to African-American U.S. Representative John Conyers. After retirement from this position, she wrote an autobiography and lived a largely private life in Detroit.

Parks eventually received many honors ranging from the 1979 Spingarn Medal to the Presidential Medal of Freedom, the Congressional Gold Medal and a posthumous statue in the United States Capitol's National Statuary Hall. Her death in 2005 was a major story in the United States' leading newspapers. She was granted the posthumous honor of lying in honor at the Capitol Rotunda.

[Wikipedia.org]

Martin Luther King, Jr. (January 15, 1929—April 4, 1968) was an American clergyman, activist, and prominent leader in the African American civil rights movement. He is best known for being an iconic figure in the advancement of civil rights in the United States and around the world, using nonviolent methods following the teachings of Mahatma Gandhi. King is often presented as a heroic leader in the history of modern American liberalism.http://en.wikipedia.org/wiki/Martin_Luther_King,_Jr. - cite_note-0

A Baptist minister, King became a civil rights activist early in his career. He led the 1955 Montgomery Bus Boycott and helped found the Southern Christian Leadership Conference in 1957, serving as its first president. King's efforts led to the 1963 March on Washington, where King delivered his "I Have a Dream" speech. There, he expanded American values to include the vision of a color blind society, and established his reputation as one of the greatest orators in American history.

In 1964, King became the youngest person to receive the Nobel Peace Prize for his work to end racial segregation and racial discrimination through civil disobedience and other nonviolent means. By the time of his death in 1968, he had refocused his efforts on ending poverty and stopping the Vietnam War.

King was assassinated on April 4, 1968, in Memphis, Tennessee. He was posthumously awarded the Presidential Medal of Freedom in 1977 and Congressional Gold Medal in 2004; Martin Luther King, Jr. Day was established as a U.S. national holiday in 1986.

[Wikipedia.org]

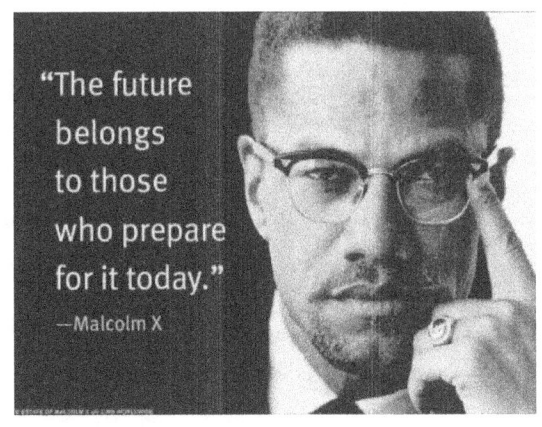

"The future belongs to those who prepare for it today."
—Malcolm X

Malcolm X (May 19, 1925—February 21, 1965), born **Malcolm Little** and also known as **El-Hajj Malik El-Shabazz** was an African-American Muslim minister, public speaker, and human rights activist. To his admirers, he was a courageous advocate for the rights of African Americans, a man who indicted white America in the harshest terms for its crimes against black Americans. His detractors accused him of preaching racism, black supremacy, anti-semitism, and violence. He has been described as one of the greatest, and most influential, African Americans in history. In 1998, *Time* named *The Autobiography of Malcolm X* one of the ten most influential nonfiction books of the 20th century.

Malcolm X was born in Omaha, Nebraska. The events of his childhood, including his father's lessons concerning black pride and self-reliance, and his own experiences concerning race, played a significant role in Malcolm X's adult life. By the time he was thirteen, his father had died and his mother had been committed to a mental hospital. After living in a series of foster homes, Malcolm X became involved in hustling and other criminal activities in Boston and New York. In 1946, Malcolm X was sentenced to eight to ten years in prison.

While in prison, Malcolm X became a member of the Nation of Islam, and after his parole in 1952, he became one of the Nation's leaders and chief spokesmen. For nearly a dozen years, he was the public face of the controversial Islamic group. Tension between Malcolm X and Elijah Muhammad, head of the Nation of Islam, led to Malcolm X's departure from the organization in March 1964. After leaving it, Malcolm X became a Sunni Muslim and made a pilgrimage to Mecca, after which he disavowed racism. He subsequently traveled extensively throughout Africa and the Middle East and then founded Muslim Mosque, Inc., a religious organization, and the secular, Pan-Africanist, Organization of Afro-American Unity. Less than a year after he left the Nation of Islam, Malcolm X was assassinated by three members of the group while giving a speech in New York.

[Wikipedia.org]

CHAPTER 8

GENERATIONS

"WE'VE COME THIS FAR BY FAITH"

by Rita G Fields
copyright 1995

LIST OF CHARACTERS

The Ferguson Family

1. Great Grandma Thelma Ferguson
2. Grandma Ann
3. Grandpa Eddie
4. Janie
5. Nat
6. Assatta
7. Paula
8. Jamel
9. Imani

Ferguson Family Tree Themes

African Ancestors

Great Grandma Thelma 1920's

Grandma Ann—Grandpa Eddie 30's—40's

Janie and Nat 50's—60's

Paula—Assatta -Jamel -70's—80's

Imani—90's

ACT I—FERGUSON FAMILY REUNION

Scene- Scene opens with O'Jays song "Family Reunion" playing. As music begins curtains open. A banner across the stage above a long picnic table says Ferguson Family Reunion.

On stage several scenes take place, i.e. family members already seated at table, food being served and eaten, relatives arriving on stage hugging each other. Around auditorium near center stage boys playing catch, girls jumping rope, students on stage right in a small group listening to music and dancing.

Families arrive through center aisles, women holding babies, pushing strollers, etc. Music fades out and Janie Ferguson comes to microphone.

JANIE: Greetings, I am Janie Ferguson. Welcome to the Ferguson family reunion 1999. It is so wonderful to see everyone. We, the Fergusons are a loving, hardworking, honest and proud family, don't you agree?

(Family members respond—shouting yeah, that's right, etc.).

JANIE: We've been meeting here in Virginia for the 5 past years. Today we would like to honor our oldest and wisest family member—Mrs. Thelma Ferguson my grandmother.

(Janie presents her with a bouquet of flowers).

MRS. THELMA FERGUSON: Thank you and welcome to you all. I'm not only the oldest but I'm the luckiest because I've been able to see almost all of you grow up. Why I use to change your diapers *(points to man, and a lady laughs)* and yours too honey *(she says to laughing lady)*. Well, bless this family, those who are here now, and those who came before us. *(She is helped by Jamel to her seat.)*

JANIE: Thank you grandma Thelma. As my grandmother stated bless those who came before us. My mind goes back to our ancestors—for those who came before us created the strong links that keep us and bring us together each year. And each year we ask Rev. Thomas to pray for us.

REVEREND THOMAS: Everybody stand please. Lord, bless the Ferguson family. May they continue their family tradition of gathering here each year—strengthening their family ties. Bless the family members who suffered, struggled and endured so that today each generation lives on in freedom. Yes lord we've come a long way and we've come this far by faith. Everybody say— Amen,

FAMILY MEMBERS: Amen.

Sing "We've Come This Far by Faith" and 2nd song.

JANIE: We have lots of activities, food and fun—so mingle and enjoy!

Family members Begin talking, playing, etc. Music begins to play "Family Reunion." Curtains close.

ACT II—AT GRANDMA & GRANDPA'S HOUSE

Room, sofa, table with books, family photo album. Entering through closed curtain in this order:

Grandpa Eddie & Grandma Thelma

Janie & Nat (Eddie's and Thelma's daughter)

Jamel & Great Grandma Ann (Jamel is Janie's younger brother)

Assatta (Janie's daughter) hold her daughters hand (Imani) and Cousin Paula.

As they enter laughing, talking.....

GRANDPA EDDIE: What a good time we had!

GRANDMA ANN: Let's all sit in the living room for awhile before we go to bed.

IMANI: Grandma what's this book about?

GREAT GRANDMA THELMA: C'mon over here child and let me tell you about your great grandma. Bring that photo album with you.

GRANDMA ANN: You know this book holds the history of our family—even my grandmother who came from Africa.

IMANI: Africa? What was Africa like great grandma Thelma?

GREAT GRANDMA THELMA: Well, I've never been to Africa sweetie pie. I don't know much about it except my mother was born there.

JAMEL: Let me tell you about Africa little sister. During the 60's when I grew up I studied all about Africa. Civilization began in Africa. Hundreds of years ago there were many great African empires ruled by *Kings.*

ASSATA: And Queens!

JAMEL: The Kingdoms of Ghana, Benin, Mali, and Songhay existed for many years.

IMANI: Real Kings and Queens?

ASSATA: Yes, there was Nandi—Queen mother of the Zulu nation.

Curtains open. Nandi stands proudly.

NARRATOR 1: Queen Nandi became a legend in the history of the Zulu people. She was the mother of Shaka, a great warrior whose military strategies are still being taught at West Point.

NARRATOR 2: Thousands paid tribute to Kings and Queens such as Kharna—Good *King* of Bechuanaland, and Nzingha—Warrior Queen of Matamba, Shamba Bolongongo—African King of Peace.

NARRATOR 3: Kings like Hannibal, Mansa Mussa and Queen Cleopatra were great noble leaders.

Music. Procession begins—Kings and Queens stroll regally down center aisle onto stage. Music stops.

King comes forward: Dancers please.

Music begins—Dancers enter from back of audience, 6 dancers in each aisle. Dance in aisles.

After dance—Dancers remain.

NARRATOR 4: Slavery was no stranger to Africa. Slave traders began to trade with Europeans. Thousands of men, women, and children were taken from their homeland to America.

Strobe light flickers.

Four boys dressed as slave traders with whips and guns enter stage. Dancers run and scream and form single lines, walking slowly. Curtains close.

IMANI: Were you a slave great grandma?

GREAT GRANDMA THELMA: No, I wasn't born then. Slavery was ended in 1865. I was born a free woman.

IMANI: Who's this lady?

GREAT GRANDMA THELMA: That's me child during my time, the 1920's. Even though anti-black groups like the Ku Klux Klan tried to keep us down using terror tactics, they couldn't hold us back.

PAULA: Great grandma, what was the 1920's like?

GREAT GRANDMA THELMA: Well it was an exciting time. I was about 19 or 20 years old living in Harlem New York.

JANIE: Here's a picture of you Grandma. Wow you look sharp.

GREAT GRANDMA THELMA: Oh yeah that was when I was stepping out—probably going to my favorite club. The 20's that was my time!

NARRATOR 5: The flowering of African American creative talent in literature, music and the arts in the 1920's was centered in Harlem, New York and this period became known as the Harlem Renaissance.

GRANDPA EDDIE: You still have some records around here don't you Thelma.

GREAT GRANDMA THELMA: These kids don't want to hear none of that old music.

They don't even know those folks.

GRANDPA EDDIE: Maybe they know about Langston Hughes. His poetry dazzled the world during the 20's and still does.

PAULA: I did a research paper on him in college. (*Turning to Imani*) Langston Hughes was a poet, but he also wrote plays, songs, and books. Langston Hughes was one of the most important writers of that period. My favorite of his poems is "Epilogue."

A student recites the poem "Epilogue. "

IMANI: Where are you going in this picture great grandma? You sure look pretty.

GREAT GRANDMA THELMA.: *(Thelma looking at picture)* Well, that's a picture of me on my 20th birthday. My friends took me to a night club called The Sugar Cane. You should've seen us. And we'd see some of the hottest shows in town.

Music plays as dressed up students stroll down aisle. Students converse as they walk. When they reach the stage curtains open to Sugar Cane nightclub scene.

Host seats guests (music stops).

ANNOUNCER: Ladies and gentlemen, welcome to the fabulous Sugar Cane Club! Have we got a show for you tonight! Here are the talented and lovely Brown Bubbling Dolls.

(Charleston music) Dancers do Charleston.

ANNOUNCER: Straight from her engagement at the fabulous Cotton Club we have a special treat for you!…—Billie Holiday!

Billie sings "Good Morning Heartache." Curtains close.

NAT (Janie's Husband): I was just a little boy then but you know who I remember during those times—Marcus Garvey! A lot of people don't know it but it was Marcus Garvey who first said Black is Beautiful, and he designed the red, black and green liberation flag. I was about 6 years old when my father took me to the most splendid parade there ever was. We had a ball. There must've been over 50,000 people singing and dancing. When the singing and dancing stopped Garvey spoke. He was a powerful speaker.

NARRATOR: Marcus Mosiah Garvey was born in Jamaica. Garvey and thousands of black people who marched with him were proud of their African heritage. They believed that Africa was a great continent and that Africans were a great people.

NARRATOR: In 1916 he left his country, the island of Jamaica. He came to the United States with a plan to build black pride and encourage black people to build a black nation in Africa. His movement was called the Back to Africa movement.

NARRATOR: Garvey was a great public speaker. He attracted millions of African people worldwide. During the 1920's Garvey and his followers marched, sang and Garvey spread the word to African Americans everywhere that they could do great things if they believed in themselves and worked together.

(Music—Caribbean) Garvey leads parade. Parade marches down aisle—carrying signs—Marcus Garvey, Africa for Africans etc. The curtains open and dancers are on stage, they dance (parade troop remain off stage). After dance and music Garvey speaks.

GARVEY: Where's the Black man's government? Where is his King and Kingdom?

Where is his President, his country, his ambassador, his army, and his men of big affairs?

As long as Africans everywhere are united, we can be successful, but divided we fall! Up you mighty people, you can accomplish what you will!

(Music) Parade and dancers leave audience through center aisle.

IMANI: *(Child looking in Family Book)* Grandma, who's this?

GRANDMA ANN: Why that's my handsome husband in uniform. I always admired you in that uniform.

IMANI: Grandpa what war did you fight in?

GRANDPA EDDIE: World War II. But unlike our troops in Saudi Arabia, back then the black soldiers overseas were separated from the white soldiers.

IMANI: But that was stupid. Weren't blacks and whites fighting for the same country?

GRANDPA EDDIE: Yes, we were, but it wasn't until 1949, 4 years after the end of World War II. The armed services decided that black people and white people could fight for our country side by side. Later on I'll show you my uniform. I think I could still fit in it.

GRANDMA ANN: *(patting grandpa's stomach)* I don't think so!

JANIE: *(holding up record)* Mama you still have all of my old records from the 50's. Remember honey we used to go to "sock hops" and remember when we won that dance contest. *(speaking to Nat)*

JAMEL: Here's a picture of y'all right here.

Janie's husband Nat grabs Janie and twirls her.

NAT: We were cool cats!

IMANI: Cool cats, how corny!

JANIE: Corny? Child, listen to this. *(She puts record on record player. Curtains open. Couples dance to 50's medley.*

PAULA: Hey Nat this looks like you. You look like you're in a singing group.

NAT: Yeah that was me. We had a group in those days—almost everybody and their brother had a group those days.

PAULA: What did you sing?

NAT: We sang what was called do-wop. During this period do-wop was a unique style of music, distinguished by its harmonizing style. We were called the "Persians." Boy did we make the girls scream. You should've seen us.

Curtains open.

ANNOUNCER: Ladies and gentlemen—The Persians singing "Closer to You" by the Channels, *(or any song from that era.)*

Do-wop group sings. Curtains close.

JANIE: Look at this Imani. Here's a picture of one of the most important days of my life.

(Shows Imani the family book. They both look at the book.)

IMANI: I know who that is. It's Dr. Martin Luther King Jr.! Was he in our family too?

JANE: No, but one of my close friends sent me this picture of her riding in the front of the bus in Montgomery Alabama. It was because of Dr. King she was able to sit anywhere in the bus she wanted to. The 1950's, my time was also the start of the civil rights movement. Black people demanded equality and dignity here in America.

IMANI: During Black History month our teacher taught us a poem by Maya Angelou, a famous African American poet. You want to hear it? Listen everybody.

Curtains open. Class recites "I Rise".

NAT: You know it's hard to imagine that just 33 years ago in many American cities black people could not vote. We could not drink from the same water fountain or use the same restrooms as white people. Black children could not go to the same schools that white children attended. Dr. King helped put an end to these injustices. Here's a picture of him in 1963 when he led the historic March on Washington, where he gave his famous "I Have A Dream" speech.

GREAT GRANDMA THELMA: Who is this with all that hair sticking up on his head, and his fist all balled up?

JAMEL: That's me! And that's not hair sticking up on my head. That's an Afro, and my fists are raised in a Black Power Salute. (*He stands raising his fist*) Many of us respected Dr. King and his theory on non-violence, but we felt that non-violence was not the answer. America recognizes power and we believed that Black people should gain political and economic power. That's why my hero was Malcolm X! He warned

America that Black people would no longer accept racial injustice.

During the 60's and 70's we did make spectacular gains in politics.

Curtains open—Achievers in single line go to mike and state achievements.

STUDENT #1: My name is Edward W. Brooke. I was elected to the Senate from Massachusetts in 1966. I was the first black Senator since 1881.

STUDENT #2: My name is Walter E. Washington. I was appointed the commissioner of Washington, D.C. in 1967.

STUDENT #3: My name is Carl Stokes. I was elected mayor of Ohio in 1967.

STUDENT #4: My name is Coleman Young. I was elected mayor of Detroit in 1973.

STUDENT #5: My name is Maynard Jackson. I was elected mayor of Atlanta in 1973.

STUDENT #6: My name is Shirley Chisholm. I was elected to the United States Congress in 1969.

STUDENT #7: My name is Patricia Roberts Harris, I was the first black woman appointed to the post of Secretary of Housing and Urban Development, 1977.

JAMEL: You know the African hairstyle and those African clothes symbolized our black pride. We were Black and Proud.

IMANI: Mommy here's a picture of us.

ASSATT A: Yeah that's us at the 1984 Democratic Convention. You were just a baby then. Jesse Jackson stepped up to that microphone and we must've applauded him for 10 minutes.

IMANI: Here we are again.

AS SATTA: Well that's us in 1988. Jesse Jackson ran an even stronger campaign to gain the Democratic nomination for President.

PAULA: He won a number of states and finished second in many others.Some people were surprised by the support he received. That was some convention. He even brought on Rosa Parks! It was historic!

JESSE JACKSON: When I look out at this convention I see the faces of America—red, yellow, brown, black, and white, we are all precious in God's sight, the real rainbow coalition. I was born in the slums, but the slums wasn't born in me! Wherever you are tonight I'm here to tell you—you can make it. Hold your head high, stick your chest out—you can make it! You must never surrender! Keep hope alive, keep hope alive, America keep hope alive! *(Convention delegates cheer.)*

NARRATOR: Jesse Jackson was the first African American male to seek the office of president but there are also many other "firsts" in African American history.

STUDENT # 1: I am Governor Douglas Wilder. I am the first African American elected governor of Virginia.

STUDENT #2: My name is David Dinkins. I am the first African American elected mayor of New York City.

STUDENT #3: My name is Shirley Chisholm. I am the first African American to be nominated for office of President.

STUDENT #4: I am Thurgood Marshall. I am the first African American judge of the United States Supreme Court,

STUDENT #5: I am Guy Bluford. I am the first African American astronaut.

STUDENT #6: My name is Fanny M. Coppin. I was born a slave, but my aunt bought my freedom for $125.00. I became one of the first black women in the United States to receive a college degree.

STUDENT #7: My name is Benjamin Banneker, I am the first African American person to receive a presidential appointment. In 1791 George Washington named me to the commission that designed the city of Washington, D.C. I am also the inventor of the clock.

STUDENT #8: My name is Marian Anderson. I am the first African American to sing a leading role at the Metropolitan Opera in New York.

STUDENT #9: My name is Colin Powell. I was born right here in the Bronx. I am the first African American to be appointed as the highest ranking official in our armed forces. I am the Chairman of the Joint Chiefs of Staff

IMANI: *(stands)* My name is Imani Ferguson. I am the first African American woman to become President.

GRANDMA ANN: It's getting late, Ms. President. Remember we got to get up and go to church tomorrow. It's the last day of the reunion.

IMANI: O.K. Goodnight grandma

GREAT GRANDMA THELMA: See these empty pages? They are for you and the next generation to fill. As you've heard, we as a people have made great achievements—your family is part of a rich and wonderful heritage. African Americans have made valuable contributions to this country.

IMANI: *(Holding book)* Wow, we've come a long way.

GRANDMA ANN: Sure did. And we've come this far by faith. Now go to bed we have church tomorrow.

Everybody says goodnight and hugs each other. Curtain is closed as one by one they disappear behind curtain. Imani is left by herself (looks around, says "Goodnight" and waves to audience).

THE END

CHAPTER 9

HISTORICAL FIGURES MENTIONED IN THE PLAY

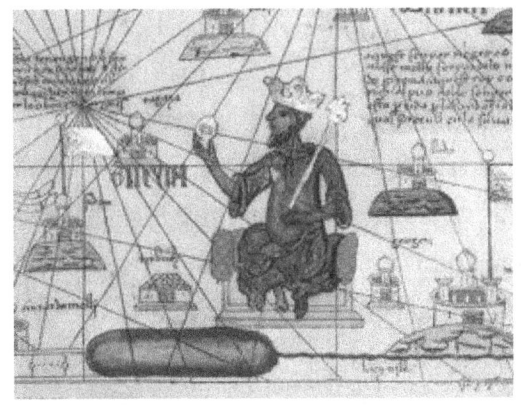

Musa I (fl. 1312—c. 1337), commonly referred to as **Mansa Musa**, was the tenth *mansa*, which translates as "king of kings" or "emperor", of the Malian Empire. At the time of Mansa Musa's rise to the throne, the Malian Empire consisted of territory formerly belonging to the Ghana Empire and Melle (Mali) and immediate surrounding areas, and Musa held many titles, including Emir of Melle, Lord of the Mines of Wangara, and conqueror of Ghanata, Futa-Jallon, and at least another dozen states. He was perhaps the wealthiest ruler of his day.

What is known about the kings of the Malian Empire is taken from the writings of Arab scholars, including Al-Umari, Abu-sa'id Uthman ad-Dukkali, Ibn Khaldun, and Ibn Battuta. According to Ibn-Khaldun's comprehensive history of the Malian kings, Mansa Musa's grandfather was Abu-Bakr (the Arabic equivalent to Bakari or Bogari, original name unknown), a brother of Sundiata Keita, the founder of the Malian Empire as recorded through oral histories.

Mansa Musa came to the throne through a practice of appointing a deputy when a king goes on his pilgrimage to Mecca or some other endeavor, and later naming the deputy as heir. According to primary sources, Musa was appointed deputy of the king before him, who had reportedly embarked on an expedition to explore the limits of the Atlantic ocean, and never returned. The Arab-Egyptian scholar Al-Umari quotes Mansa Musa as follows: "The ruler who preceded me did not believe that it was impossible to reach the extremity of the ocean that encircles the earth (meaning the Atlantic). He wanted to reach that (end) and was determined to pursue his plan. So he equipped two hundred boats full of men, and many others full of gold, water and provisions sufficient for several years. He ordered the captain not to return until they had reached the other end of the ocean, or until he had exhausted the provisions and water. So they set out on their journey. They were absent for a long period, and, at last just one boat returned. When questioned, the captain replied: 'O Prince, we navigated for a long period, until we saw in the midst of the ocean a great river which flowing massively. My boat was the last one; others were ahead of me, and they were drowned in the great whirlpool and never came out again. I sailed back to escape this current.' But the Sultan would not believe him. He ordered two thousand boats to be equipped for him and his men, and one thousand more for water and provisions. Then he conferred the regency on me for the term of his absence, and departed with his men, never to return nor to give a sign of life".

[WIKIPEDIA.ORG]

Marcus Mosiah Garvey, Jr., (17 August 1887—10 June 1940) was a publisher, journalist, entrepreneur, Black Nationalist, Pan-Africanist, and orator. Marcus Garvey was founder of the Universal Negro Improvement Association and African Communities League (UNIA-ACL). Prior to the twentieth century, leaders such as Prince Hall, Martin Delany, Edward Wilmot Blyden, and Henry Highland Garnet advocated the involvement of the African diaspora in African affairs. Garvey was unique in advancing a Pan-African philosophy to inspire a global mass movement focusing on Africa known as Garveyism Promoted by the UNIA as a movement of *African Redemption*, Garveyism would eventually inspire others, ranging from the Nation of Islam, to the Rastafari movement (which proclaims Garvey as a prophet). The intention of the movement was for those of African ancestry to "redeem" Africa. His essential ideas about Africa were stated in an editorial in the *Negro World* titled "African Fundamentalism" where he wrote: Our union must know no clime, boundary, or nationality…let us hold together under all climes and in every country

As a young man of fourteen, Garvey left school and worked as a printer's apprentice. He participated in Jamaica's earliest nationalist organizations, traveled throughout Central America, and spent time in London, England, where he worked with the Sudanese-Egyptian nationalist Duse Mohamed Ali. In 1916 Garvey was invited by Booker T. Washington to come to the United States in the hopes of establishing an industrial training school, but arrived just after Washington died. In March 1916, shortly after landing in America, Garvey embarked upon an extended period of travel. When he finally settled down, he organized a chapter of the Universal Negro Improvement Association and African Communities League. The UNIA & ACL had been formed in Jamaica in 1914. Its motto was "One God, One Aim, One Destiny," and pledged itself to the redemption of Africa and the uplift of Black people everywhere. It aimed at race pride, self-reliance and economic independence.

[Africawithin.com; Wikipedia.org]

Thurgood Marshall

Thurgood Marshall photographed in 1967 in the Oval Office Born in Baltimore, Maryland on July 2, 1908, Thurgood Marshall was the grandson of a slave. His father, William Marshall, instilled in him from youth an appreciation for the United States Constitution and the rule of law. After completing high school in 1925, Thurgood followed his brother, William Aubrey Marshall, at the historically black Lincoln University in Chester County, Pennsylvania. His classmates at Lincoln included a distinguished group of future Black leaders such as the poet and author Langston Hughes, the future President of Ghana, Kwame Nkrumah, and musician Cab Calloway. Just before graduation, he married his first wife, Vivian "Buster" Burey. Their twenty-five year marriage ended with her death from cancer in 1955.

June 13, 1967, President Johnson appointed Marshall to the Supreme Court following the retirement of Justice Tom C. Clark, saying that this was "the right thing to do, the right time to do it, the right man and the right place." Marshall was confirmed as an Associate Justice by a Senate vote of 69-11 on August 30, 1967. He was the 96th person to hold the position, and the first African-American. President Johnson confidently predicted to one biographer, Doris Kearns Goodwin, that a lot of black baby boys would be named "Thurgood" in honor of this choice. Marshall served on the Court for the next twenty-four years

[WIKIPEDIA.ORG]

Shirley Chisholm

Shirley St. Hill Chisholm was born on November 30, 1924 in Brooklyn, New York to Charles and Ruby St. Hill. In 1964 Chisholm ran for a state assembly seat. She won and served in the New York General Assembly from 1964 to 1968. During her tenure in the legislature, she proposed a bill to provide state aid to day-care centers and voted to increase funding for schools on a per-pupil basis. In 1968, After finishing her term in the legislature, Chisholm campaigned to represent New York's Twelfth Congressional District. Her campaign slogan was "Fighting Shirley Chisholm— Unbought and Unbossed." She won the election and became the first African American woman elected to Congress.

During her first term in Congress, Chisholm hired an all-female staff and spoke out for civil rights, women's rights, the poor and against the Vietnam War. In 1970, she was elected to a second term. She was a sought-after public speaker and cofounder of the National Organization for Women (NOW). She remarked that, "Women in this country must become revolutionaries. We must refuse to accept the old, the traditional roles and stereotypes."

On January 25, 1972, Chisholm announced her candidacy for president. She stood before the cameras and in the beginning of her speech she said,

"I stand before you today as a candidate for the Democratic nomination for the Presidency of the United States. I am not the candidate of black America, although I am black and proud. I am not the candidate of the women's movement of this country, although I am a woman, and I am equally proud of that. I am not the candidate of any political bosses or special interests. I am the candidate of the people."

[WIKIPEDIA.ORG]

Maynard Jackson

Maynard Holbrook Jackson, Jr. (March 23, 1938—June 23, 2003) was an American politician, a member of the Democratic Party, and the first African American mayor of Atlanta, Georgia. He served three terms, two consecutive terms from 1974 until 1982 and a third term from 1990 to 1994. He became the first African-American mayor of Atlanta in the same week that Coleman Young became the first African-American mayor of Detroit.

Jesse Jackson

Born October 8, 1941, Greenville, South Carolina, U.S.) American civil rights leader, Baptist minister, and politician whose bids for the U.S. presidency (in the Democratic Party's nomination races in 1983–84 and 1987–88) were the most successful by an African American until 2008, when Barack Obama captured the Democratic presidential nomination. Jackson's life and career have been marked by both accomplishment and controversy.

While an undergraduate, Jackson became involved in the civil rights movement. In 1965 he went to Selma, Alabama, to march with Martin Luther King, Jr., and became a worker in King's Southern Christian Leadership Conference (SCLC). Jackson helped found the Chicago branch of Operation Breadbasket, the economic arm of the SCLC, in 1966 and served as the organization's national director from 1967 to 1971. He was in Memphis, Tennessee, with King when the civil rights leader was assassinated on April 4, 1968, though his exact location at the moment King was shot has long been a matter of controversy. Accused of using the SCLC for personal gain, Jackson was suspended by the organization, whereupon he formally resigned in 1971 and founded Operation PUSH (People United to Save Humanity), a Chicago-based organization in which he advocated black self-help and achieved a broad audience for his liberal views. In 1984 he established the National Rainbow Coalition, which sought equal rights for African Americans, women, and homosexuals. These two organizations merged in 1996 to form the Rainbow/PUSH Coalition.

[Wikipedia.org]

 BROOKE, Edward William, III, a Senator from Massachusetts; born in Washington, D.C., October 26, 1919; attended the public schools of Washington, D.C.; graduated from Howard University, Washington, D.C., in 1941; graduated, Boston University Law School 1948; captain, United States Army, infantry, with five years of active service in the European theater of operations; chairman of Finance Commission, city of Boston 1961-1962; elected attorney general of the Commonwealth of Massachusetts in 1962; reelected in 1964; elected as a Republican to the United States Senate in 1966; reelected in 1972 and served from January 3, 1967, to January 3, 1979; unsuccessful candidate for reelection in 1978; first African American elected to the Senate by popular vote; lawyer; awarded the Presidential Medal of Freedom on June 23, 2004; is a resident of Miami, Fla.

[Wikipedia.org]

Coleman Young (May 24, 1918-Nov. 29, 1997)

Coleman Young was the first black mayor of Detroit and one of the first black mayors of any major American city. He moved to Detroit with his family as a youngster and later worked at Ford Motors, where he was fired for being a labor union organizer. During World War II he served as a navigator with the Tuskegee Airmen. Young was elected to the Michigan state senate in 1964 (serving from 1965-73), joined the Democratic National Committee in 1968, and in 1973 was elected mayor of Detroit. He was the city's mayor for the next 20 years, retiring in 1993 after five terms. Young's brash charm and plainspoken style made him something of a folk hero, especially to Detroit's many African-American citizens, and Michigan's role as a major electoral state made him a power broker in national politics as well. He published *Hard Stuff: The Autobiography of Coleman Young* in 1994.

[Wikipedia.org]

Carl Burton Stokes (June 21, 1927–April 3, 1996) was an American politician of the Democratic party who served as the 51st mayor of Cleveland, Ohio. Elected on November 7, 1967, but took office on Jan 1, 1968, he was the first African American mayor of a major U.S. city.

Elected to the Ohio House of Representatives in 1962, he served 3 terms. Stokes worked hard to even out legislative districts during that time since Ohio had uneven representation among its Congressional and General Assembly districts. By the late 1960s, he was able to carve out a district that could elect him to Congress, but deferred to his brother Louis Stokes who represented Cleveland in the U.S. House of Representatives for three decades. Stokes narrowly lost a bid for mayor of Cleveland in 1965. His victory two years later drew national attention, as he was the first African-American mayor of one of the ten biggest cities in the United States. Able to mobilize both black and white voters, he defeated Seth Taft, the grandson of a former U.S. president, with a 50.5 majority

[Wikipedia.org]

Benjamin Banneker *mathematician, astronomer, surveyor*

Born: 11/9/1731

Birthplace: Ellicott's Mills, Md.

Benjamin Banneker was born in Maryland on November 9, 1731. His father and grandfather were former slaves. A farmer of modest means, Banneker nevertheless lived a life of unusual achievement. In 1753, the young man borrowed a pocket watch from a well-to-do neighbor; he took it apart and made a drawing of each component, then reassembled the watch and returned it, fully functioning, to its owner.

From his drawings Banneker then proceeded to carve, out of wood, enlarged replicas of each part. Calculating the proper number of teeth for each gear and the necessary relationships between the gears, he constructed a working wooden clock that kept accurate time and struck the hours for over 50 years.

At age 58, Banneker began the study of astronomy and was soon predicting future solar and lunar eclipses. He compiled the ephemeris, or information table, for annual almanacs that were published for the years 1792 through 1797. "Benjamin Banneker's Almanac" was a top seller from Pennsylvania to Virginia and even into Kentucky.

. It is believed to be the first scientific book published by an African American. Also a surveyor and mathematician, Banneker was appointed by President George Washington to the District of Columbia Commission, which was responsible for the survey work that established the city's original boundaries. When the chairman of the committee, Pierre Charles L'Enfant, suddenly resigned and left, taking the plans with him, Banneker reproduced the plans from memory, saving valuable time. A staunch opponent of slavery, Banneker sent a copy of his first almanac to then-Secretary of State Thomas Jefferson to counter Jefferson's belief in the intellectual inferiority of blacks.

[Wikipedia.org]

Sojourner Truth (c1797—November 26, 1883) was the self-given name, from 1843, of **Isabella Baumfree**, an African-American abolitionist and women's rights activist. Truth was born into slavery in Swarte kill, New York.

On June 1, 1843, Truth changed her name to *Sojourner Truth* and told her friends, "The Spirit calls me, and I must go." She became a Methodist, and left to make her way traveling and preaching about abolition. In 1844, she joined the Northampton Association of Education and Industry in Northampton, Massachusetts. Founded by abolitionists, the organization supported women's rights and religious tolerance as well as pacifism. There were 210 members and they lived on 500 acres (2 km²), raising livestock, running a sawmill, a gristmill, and a silk factory. While there, Truth met William Lloyd Garrison, Frederick Douglass, and David Ruggles.

Her best-known speech, Ain't I a Woman?, was delivered in 1851 at the Ohio Women's Rights Convention in Akron, Ohio.

"That man over there says that women need to be helped into carriages, and lifted over ditches, and to have the best place everywhere. Nobody ever helps me into carriages, or over mud puddles, or gives me any best place, and ain't I a woman?…I have plowed, and planted, and gathered into bar ns, and no man could head me—and ain't I a woman? I could work as much and eat as much as a man (when I could get it), and bear the lash as well—and ain't I a woman? I have borne thirteen children and seen most all sold off to slavery and when I cried out with my mother's grief, none but Jesus heard me—and ain't I a woman?"

During the Civil War Sojourner Truth raised food and clothing contributions for black regiments, and met Abraham Lincoln at the White House in 1864. While there, she tried to challenge the discrimination that segregated street cars by race.

After the War ended, Sojourner Truth again spoke widely, advocating for some time a "Negro State" in the west. She spoke mainly to white audiences, and mostly on religion, "Negro" and women's rights, and on temperance, though immediately after the Civil War she tried to organize efforts to provide jobs for black refugees from the war.

[Wikipedia.org]

Lewis Howard Latimer

(September 4, 1848—December 11, 1928) was an African American inventor and draftsman.

Lewis Howard Latimer was born in Chelsea, Massachusetts on September 4 1848 as the youngest of the four children of Rebecca (1826-1848) and George Latimer (July 4, 1818 c.1880). George Latimer had been the slave of James B. Gray of Virginia. George Latimer ran away to freedom in Trenton, New Jersey in October, 1842, along with his wife Rebecca, who had been the high slave of another man. When Gray, the owner, appeared in Boston to take them back to Virginia, it became a noted case in the movement for abolition of slavery, gaining the involvement of such abolitionists as William Lloyd Garrison. Eventually funds were raised to pay Gray $400 for the freedom of George Latimer. Lewis Latimer joined the U.S. Navy at the age of 15 on September 16, 1863. After receiving an honorable discharge from the Navy on July 3, 1865, he gained employment as an office boy with a patent law firm, *Crosby Halstead and Gould*, with a $3.00 per week salary. He learned how to use an L square, ruler, and other tools. Later, after his boss recognized his talent for sketching patent drawings, Latimer was promoted to the position of head draftsman earning $20.00 a week by 1878.[1] In 1874, he co- patented (with Charles W. Brown) an improved toilet system for railroad cars called the Water Closet for Railroad Cars (U.S. Patent 147,363).

In 1876, Alexander Graham Bell employed Latimer, then a draftsman at Bell's patent law firm, to draft the necessary drawings required to receive a patent for Bell's telephone.[2]

In 1879, he moved to Bridgeport, Connecticut with his brother, William, his mother, Rebecca, and his wife. Lewis was hired as assistant manager and draftsman for the U.S. Electric Lighting Company, a company owned by Hiram Maxim, a rival inventor of Thomas Edison. Latimer received a patent in January 1881 for the "Process of Manufacturing Carbons", an improved method for the production of carbon filaments for light bulb. The Edison Electric Light Company in New York City hired Latimer in 1884, as a draftsman and an expert witness in patent litigation on electric lights.

[Wikipedia.org]

Colin Luther Powell (pronounced /ˈkoʊlɪn/; born April 5, 1937) is an American statesman and a retired four-star general in the United States Army. He was the 65th United States Secretary of State (2001–2005), serving under President George W. Bush. He was the first African American appointed to that position. During his military career, Powell also served as National Security Advisor (1987–1989), as Commander of the U.S. Army Forces Command (1989) and as Chairman of the Joint Chiefs of Staff (1989–1993), holding the latter position during the Gulf War. He was the first, and so far the only, African American to serve on the Joint Chiefs of Staff.

[Wikipedia.org]

CHAPTER 10

MR. READ

By Rita G. Fields

CAST OF CHARACTERS:

WIFE, Mrs. Jones

HUSBAND, Mr. Jones

DAUGHTER

SECRETARY

:MR. JACOBS

NARRATOR #1, Librarian's Daughter

BOY #1

BOY #2,

LIBRARIAN

CHILD IN LIBRARY

EDDIE

MR. READ

ACT I

SCENE I

(CURTAINS OPEN: WIFE IS COOKING AND PREPARING BREAKFAST.

HUSBAND ENTERS ROOM AND SITS AT TABLE.)

MRS. JONES: Good morning dear. I'm surprised to see you up so early. You tossed and turned all night.

MR. JONES: Yeah. I had a nightmare that a big computerized elevator chased me and ate me up.

MRS. JONES: You probably have losing your job still on your mind. I know you liked your job so much. You were the best elevator operator in New York City. Why did they have to put in those self-operating elevators after all these years. Now you're out of a job and things are so hard. I don't know how we're going to make it.

(Starts crying) (Sits at table)

MR. JONES: Don't worry dear. I have an interview this morning downtown. Last night Mr. Thomas came over to tell me they need an elevator engineer in his office building, so he set up an appointment for me. Don't worry, our troubles will be over because this job will pay much more than my elevator operator job.

(DAUGHTER ENTERS AND SITS AT TABLE)

DAUGHTER: Good morning, Dad. If don't bring in sneakers for gym, the instructor said I'd fail. I really need some sneakers or I'll fail.

FATHER: Look, things are a little tough right now. We're short of money.

DAUGHIER: We're always short on money. I'm going to fail! It's not fair! (Runs out of room crying)

(WIFE COMES OVER AND PATS HUSBAND'S BACK) Don't feel bad dear, she doesn't understand things like this.

HUSBAND: Yeah. Where's Bobby?

WIFE: He left early. He had to be at the supermarket by 7:30. He got a little part-time job to help out.

HUSBAND: But he has to go to school! Nothing comes before his education. You know how strongly I feel about that!

WIFE: Calm down. It's from 7:30 to 8:30 and his first class starts at 8:40. The school is right around the comer from the supermarket; he gets to school on time. After school, he works from 4 to 6. Besides, we can use the extra money and sometimes his boss gives him meat and food to bring home. Bobby feels good. He wants to help. I make sure it doesn't interfere with his school work.

HUSBAND: I don't want anything (bangs table) to interfere with his class work!

(WIFE COMES OVER AND PATS HUSBAND'S BACK)

HUSBAND: If I had only felt this way when I was going to school.

WIFE: (PUTS ON HER COAT) Well, I promised my boss I'd be in early. I have to run. Good luck on the interview.

(WIFE LEAVES)

MR. JONES: (TALKING TO AUDIENCE) Things sure do look bad for me, don't they? My daughter needs sneakers, my son has to work before and after school. I have to get that job this morning. I know I'm qualified. I just hope I don't have to fill out any…or worst than that, take a…I'm too embarrassed to tell you now. Just wish me luck, I'll need it!

(CURTINS CLOSE)

SCENE II

(MR. JONES ENTERS OFFICE OF SECRETARY. SHE IS ON TELEPHONE)

SECRETARY: Yes, yes, he'll be available at 10:00 sharp. (Hangs up) May I help you sir?

MR. JONES: Yes! I have a 9:00 appointment with Mr. Jacobs.

SECRETARY: (CHECKS APPOINTMENT BOOK) Yes. You must be Mr. Jones. What position are you applying for?

MR. JONES: Elevator Engineer.

SECRETARY: Could you have a seat and fill out these papers?

MR. JONES: Ah, Ah, papers for what?

SECRETARY: It's just an application. (Buzzer rings. Mr. Jacobs says send him right in.) One second. (She talks on phone as Mr. Jones acts and looks nervous) You can fill these papers in later. Mr. Jacobs wants to see you now. (Mr. Jones wipes forehead with handkerchief; looks very relieved)

SCENE II
(MR. JONES SITS AT DESK)

MR. JACOBS: Good morning. So you're interested in the position as elevator engineer? (Shakes hands) Why do you think you're the man for the job?

MR. JONES: Well, I know all there is about elevators. I've been an elevator operator for 10 years. I started at Gracy's Department store and was promoted to their executive office building as foreman. I ran elevators. I operated elevators and was in charge of 10 other operators. I've experienced probably every emergency possible and I am capable of handling any problem or emergency.

MR. JACOBS: So, Why did you leave?

MR. JONES: I was replaced by self-service elevators. You know, they had to move with the times, I guess.

MR. JACOBS: But didn't your company still need someone to monitor the elevators? They do break down now and then. Why didn't they keep you?

MR. JONES: Well, they have computers that make sure the elevators run smoothly and an outside maintenance company handles emergencies.

MR. JACOBS: Well we need a man here, although our elevators are self-service, with all the modem equipment, but we need someone here on the premises to monitor the elevator banks, and also to take care of any problems that may come up. (Starts laughing) Get it? Any problems that might come up!

MR JONES: Yeah. (Laughs phony)

MR. JACOBS: I prefer a man with experience like yourself. You can always learn the rest by reading a few manuals I'll give you. (Mr. Jones looks nervous) If you want the job it's yours.

MR. JONES: I want it. Thank you sir! Now, what about reading some manuals?

MR. JACOBS: Well, there are a few things about our company and about the elevator system you'll be in charge of; You know, all the technical and mechanical details you'll have to learn. You look a little worried. Oh. Your salary! You'll be making twice as much as you did on your previous job. Welcome to our company! (Buzzes secretary) Mrs. Smith, please give Mr. Jones the service manuals and take care of him.

(Mr. Jones leaves office; goes to Mrs. Smith's desk)

SECRETARY: Here are the manuals you'll need to read. And before you leave, could you fill out these papers? (Mr. Jones looks very nervous)

MR. JONES: Why?

SECRETARY: Why? Well, we need information, references for our personnel file. You know, the usual. I'll leave you alone to fill them out. (*SHE LEAVES ROOM*)

MR. JONES: (SITS AT DESK, LOOKING AT PAPERS. HE LOOKS FRUSTRATED; THROWS PENCIL DOWN) (HE SPEAKS TO AUDIENCE)

"I should be happy right? I should be overjoyed! But you know what? I blew this job just like I blew my old job. They asked me to stay on. All I would have to do is read and update myself on the new systems. But I couldn't. And as bad as I need this job, I can't take it. Why? It's these papers, this manual! (Throws them down; then looks sadly at them and picks them up) No! It's not them. It's me. *I can't read*!" (Hangs head sadly)

NARRATOR # 1: Good morning Principal, assistant principals, teachers, and fellow students. Mr. Jones here is one of the millions of Americans who are classified as illiterate. Illiterate means unable to read and write. It's hard to believe, but there are so many people like Mr. Jones who cannot read or write. Some of these people are able to go through life, even holding jobs. We call these people "functional illiterates." They are able to 'get by' or function without being able to read or write. The reason I know so much about this subject is because my mother is the librarian at our neighborhood library. She also teach classes that instruct many illiterates and functional illiterates. Maybe she can help Mr. Jones. I'll ask him to come to the library with me. (She walks over to him and they begin to talk, and then they begin to walk to the library.)

SCENE IV

(TWO BOYS COME DOWN THE STREET DRESSED IN BASKETBALL GEAR DRIBBLING BALL; ONE OF THE BOYS HAS 2 BOOKS TUCKED UNDER HIS ARM.)

BOY#l: (RUNNING, DRIBBLING BALL) C'mon let's go to the park for awhile!

BOY #2: No, man. I have to get to the library. I want to check out some books.

BOY # 1: Oh, that's no fun. We can have a ball at the park.

BOY #2: Well, I've been reading about a lot of basketball champions, and if I'm going to be a pro one day, I have to keep my grades up as well as my reading scores. Not only basketball players, but many other professional athletes are selected from colleges all around the country. Guys like Michael Jordan, Shaquille O'Neal and Reggie Miller, not only had to be skilled at playing their game, but their reading skills had to be good in order to understand some of those magnificent plays they had to read and study and practice. Anyway, I want to know anything and everything about basketball because after I can't play anymore, I want to be a coach. So reading is the answer for me.

BOY # 1: Sounds good! Maybe I'll go to the library with you!

BOY # 2: (SHOWING BOOK TO HIS FRIEND) I'm returning this book. It was **bad**! It even told how the first basketball game (They walk to the library)

SCENE V

(AT THE LIBRARY. BOOKS PILED ON DESK; LIBRARIAN BEHIND DESK; BOY COMES TO DESK LOADED WITH BOOKS.)

LIBRARIAN: EDDIE, you won't be able to take out all of these books today. Why don't you read these 3 and come back for more when you're finished?

EDDIE: AW, OK. But I'll probably be back before you know it. I don't know which 3 to take out (picks up book) I think I'll take these three. No. No. Let me take the Tom Sawyer; no. Encyclope-dia Brown..... {Librarian and boy talk among themselves)

(THE TWO BASKETBALL PLAYING BOYS, NARRATOR, AND MR. JONES ARRIVE)

LIBRARIAN'S DAUGHTER: Mother, I want you to meet Mr. Jones. He is interested in attending the library's reading classes.

LIBRARIAN: Glad to meet you Mr. Jones. You are doing the right thing. Reading is so important to our everyday lives and it's never, ever too late to learn. Reading is just too important. (VOICE FROM NO WHERE) "HOW IMPORTANT IS IT? (LIBRARIAN LOOKS SHOCKED; FINDS KID AND POINTS TO "QUIET" SIGN) Well,..... (Mr. Jones interrupts)

MR JONES: Children, I guess no one knows better than I do how important reading is. Being unable to read has really affected my life in a bad way. Many times, being unable to read has pre-vented me or even kept me from trying to do many things. Like today, I could've gotten a good paying job that would've allowed me to support me and my family much better. But to learn how to operate some of the new equipment on my job, I would have to be able to read a book that would instruct me. Even worse, I couldn't fill out the job application.

CHILD IN LIBRARY: But how do you get around?

MR. JONES: I memorize the way. And if I'm driving, I can't read the road signs, so a lot of times, I've gotten lost. Once I got very sick because I couldn't read the directions on my medication and took more medicine than I should have. It's terrible. I could go on and on. But what I'm trying to say is that reading is like a key. It opens doors for you. Doors that are closed to me. It opens the doors to understanding the world you live in. It opens the doors to a good career, and a better you!

LIBRARIAN: (COMES OVER CLAPPING) Well put. I must add something. As Mr. Jones said, life can be difficult if you do not know how to read. And just like double Dutch, and basketball, the more you practice the better you get. Well the same goes for reading. The more you read, the more you are using and sharpening the skills you were taught. And boy do we have good books for you! Did anyone read a good book lately? (CHILDREN RAISE HANDS AND GIVE ORAL BOOK REPORTS) CHILD: I love to read, but when my teacher says do a book report I really find it a drag!

GIRL: A drag! Reporting on a book can be fun. You just have to use your imagination.

(CHILDREN TELL ABOUT TIIE VARIOUS TYPES OF BOOK REPORTS, i.e., MOBILE, DIORAMA, THUMBNAIL REPORT, BOOK JACKET REPORT)

CHILD: HEY! It doesn't have to be a drag.

LIBRARIAN: Remember, practice, practice, practice. Read, read, read!

CHILD: You can start right now by joining C.E. S. 70'S reading club.

(LOTS OF NOISE AND COMMOTION BEGIN)

LIBRARIAN: who is making all that noise!!

CHILD: It's MR. Read!! Hold on to your books!'

MR. JONES: Who is Mr. Read?

CHILD: Mr. Read? Why, he likes to read everything and anything. He's the best reader in the world!

(ENTER MR. READ—LOOKS LIKE MR.T)

MR. READ: I heard something about a Reading Club! How come I didn't know about a Reading Club? Somebody tell me something quick!

CHILD: (NERVOUSLY) I was just telling the kids about C.E.S. 70'S Reading Club.

MR. READ: I want to join. What do I need to do?

CHILD: Just read a book. (Mr. Read takes a kid's book) Write a book report on it and then write down 10 questions on the book and then do an art project.

MR. READ: That's it?! Do I get anything?'

CHILD: Yes. You will get a certificate, and when we start contests, the child (she looks at Mr. Read), or member who has read the most books can win a prize.

MR. READ: Sounds good. Good move—C.E.S. 70'S Reading Club- Give me that book (grabs book)! I read that one already!

MR JONES: Well, I'm going to learn to read and write, finally. But I must say, you (points to audience) are lucky. You are way ahead of the game. You know the importance of getting an education and learning to read or else you wouldn't be sitting here. But keep up the good work. Do as much reading as you can. Be prepared for what life has to offer you.

MR. READ: HEY! BE QUIET. THIS IS A LIBRARY.

MR JONES: I was just saying how important it is to be able to read.

MR. READ: Oh, that's right. I PITTY THE FOOL WHO DON'T THINK READING IS IMPORTANT! I feel like rapping about reading.

SCENE VI

(music—READING RAP)

MR. READ: I'm MR. READ, and I'm asking you to take my advice, So, whatever you do, please listen to me and think about it twice. Make sure **you read and study** everyday, before you run out to play

Because when you read, you will succeed—and make your future a better day.

You can be a **doctor, lawyer, teacher, singer, anything,** yes **indeed!**

But in order for you to reach your goals or get the job, you must know how to **read!**

(repeat) **YOU MUST KNOW HOW TO READ!**

THE END

copyright 1995

CHAPTER II

SHINING STAR AWARDS SHOW

A PLAY

By Rita G. Fields
Copyright 1995

CAST OF CHARACTERS
(*indicates award receipients)

NARRATOR 1

NARRATOR 2

AFRICAN DANCERS (8)

BILL COSBY

WHITNEY HOUSTON

PHYLICIA RASHAD

*DR. MAE JEMISON

KADEEM HARDISON

*MAYA ANGELOU

*KRIS KROSS

SUPER CAT

KRISS KROSS DANCERS (6)

CICILY TYSON

*MARVA COLLINS

MAYOR DINKINS

FERNANDO FERRER

*DR. LORRAINE HALE

*ARTHUR MITCHELL

DANCE THEATRE OF HARLEM DANCERS (8-10)

GREGORY HINES

ARSENIO HALL

*MICHAEL JORDAN

SPIKE LEE

*OPRAH WINFREY

EDDIE MURPHY

JASMINE GUY

*MICHAEL JACKSON

SCENE I (CURTAINS CLOSED)

NARRATOR 1: Welcome to CES70'S first African-American Achievement Awards show. Here to welcome you are the fabulous Larogue Bey Dancers from Harlem, USA performing a West African welcoming dance—"Funga Alafiyah Ashay Ashay—We welcome you, one and all!

(music: Funga—dancers enter from rear of audience center aisle, performs welcoming dance) (curtains close)

NARRATOR 2: And now the hosts of our show—he was the star of two of the longest running television sitcoms on television—"I Spy" and "The Cosby Show," comedian, social activist, movie star—Bill Cosby. *(Bill comes from stage left to center stage)*

Bill's co-host is hailed as one of the best singers and entertainers of our time, and now adds actress to the list of her achievements—the lovely and talented Whitney Houston! *(Whitney enters stage right—to center stage—walks with Bill to podium).*

BILL COSBY: Whitney you look so beautiful tonight I think you may need a bodyguard *for real.*

WHITNEY: Thanks, Bill- and if I might add, you look mighty fine yourself *(Bill makes a funny, shy face).*

BILL: Well this evening we're here to honor many special African Americans. Tonight we will award those African Americans who have in some way made our world a better place.

WHITNEY: That's right Bill, tonight we want to recognize African Americans who used their talents, skills, courage and creativity to educate, help, and entertain others. Because they brighten the world and outshine all others they will be awarded with this *(holds up the shining star trophy)*—the Shining Star Award.

BILL: We will recognize those who are prominent in several fields and whose special achievements or contributions in that field are outstanding—so let's present our first Shining Star Award in the field of Science. Here to present the Shining Star in Science is the lovely and talented actress who played my wife Claire Huxtable—Phylicia Rashad.

PHYLICIA: In August 1987, Dr. Mae Jemison, a young doctor in Los Angeles was chosen as an astronaut candidate. Mae Jemison had been chosen from nearly 2,000 applicants as one of the 15 members of NASA's 1987 astronaut training program. She traveled into space in August, 1992 on Space Lab J, making her the world's first African American female astronaut. This Shining Star in Science goes to Dr. Mae Jemison – African American astronaut.

DR. JEMISON: The most important challenge in my life is to always test the limits of my abilities, do the best job I can at the time, while remaining true to myself. Thank you for this wonderful award.

WHITNEY: Our next award will be given to a shining star in the field of Literature—here to present the award is the very talented star of "A Different World"—you know him as Dwayne Wayne—but he's really Kadeem Hardison!

KADEEM: The recipient of the Shining Star award in Writing is a remarkable woman who suffered a difficult and unhappy childhood. For 5 years she could not even speak. But with the love and support of her grandmother and brother she slowly overcame her fears. Maya Angelou, born Marguerite Johnson, is an author, poet, songwriter, dancer, actor, director, and producer. She's been nominated for a Tony Award for acting, a Pulitzer Prize for poetry and a national book award for her autobiography I Know Why The Caged Bird Sings which was made into a television movie. The recipient of the Shining Star Award in Literature goes to Maya Angelou.

MAYA: Thank you so much for this special award. When I was a little girl I read a lot. Through my reading I learned that my people have a rich and wonderful history. When I was a little girl I had to find out about how great my people were on my own, because in my school books they didn't tell us about any good things that African Americans did. That is why I wrote this poem entitled "I Rise. "

You may write me down in history

With your bitter, twisted lies,

You may trod me in the very dirt

But still, like dust, I'll rise, I'll rise

I'll rise!

Thank you once again.

BILL COSBY: Our next award category is New Performing Artists. It has been said that music is the universal message, the glue that holds the world together. Before we give our next award we'd like to present 2 young men who have broken records with their smash hit. Ladies and Gentlemen, Kriss-Kross performing with Super Cat—Jump! Jump!

(Kris-Kross perform song and dance)

BILL COSBY: The Shining Star awards goes to Kriss Kross for best new performing artists.

KRISS KROSS: We'd like to thank our parents and managers and our fans. This is like a dream come true for us. Stay in school, study hard, follow your dreams—they can come true. Peace!

BILL: Our next award is given in the field of education. Presenting that award is a woman who has portrayed many heroic women on stage, screen, and television, the gifted and talented Cicely Tyson.

CICELY: Whatever good I have accomplished as an actress, I believe came in direct proportion to my efforts to portray African American women who have made positive contributions to my heritage. I had the privilege of portraying the recipient of this award, for she has given so much. Frustrated with the educational system that she worked in as a public school teacher for 14 years, Marva Collins retired from her teaching job and opened her own school, Westside Preparatory. She started off with only 18 students including her own children. But her class quickly grew as she became known for teaching children who could not be reached by other teachers. Today teachers from all over the world visit her school to learn about Marva's successful teaching methods. That is why The Shining Star in Education is given to a devoted teacher—Marva Nettles Collins!

MARVA: I truly love teaching and learning. In my school we have a motto: Entrance to learn—exit to serve. We teach our children to believe in themselves. I say this to all of my students: Some will tell you that it cannot be done, some will tell you that you will fail. But only you will know how far you can sail. So say to yourself, "I shall not fail." You are the future. Thank you!

BILL: My co-host believes that children are the future too. Here's Whitney singing "The Greatest Love of All. "

(Whitney sings)

BILL COSBY: Our next award will be presented by the first African American Mayor of New York City—Mayor David Dinkins, and the first Puerto Rican Borough President, Bronx Borough President Fernando Ferrar.

MAYOR DINKINS: The next Shining Star will be given to a humanitarian. A human being who goes beyond the call of duty to help others. Clara McBride Hale was such a person. When Clara's husband died, leaving her with a son and daughter to care for, she started making her living watching other people's children for them while they worked. Some of the children didn't want to leave Clara's home, so she kept them and raised them as her own. Over the years she raised 40 children and sent them all to college. Many are doctors, lawyers, and teachers. In 1969 her daughter sent her a drug addicted single mother and her baby. Clara took care of the mother and the baby. Soon she had 22 addicted babies living in her 5 room apartment.

FERRER: The number didn't stop at 22. Soon Clara was able to expand her service to babies whose mothers were addicted to drugs and now to babies infected with the deadly disease AIDS. Over 600 addicted babies have been cared for at Hale House, a brownstone right here in Harlem,

New York. Hundreds of children have returned to health after being cared for and loved by Clara McBride Hale—affectionately known as Mother Hale. In 1985, President Ronald Reagan cited her as an American hero. Mother Hale died last year, but the good work she started is still being carried on at Hale House by her daughter, Dr. Lorraine Hale. For her dedication to helping others we present The Shining Star award to Mother Hale. Her daughter will accept the award.

LORRAINE HALE: I remember growing up in a house full of children and full of love. My mother Clara Hale said these words—Until I die, I'm going to keep doing. My people need me. I'm not an American hero. I'm a person who loves children. I accept this award for my mother—and mom, if you're listening, you are a hero. Thank you.

(Bill goofing around, dancing)

WHITNEY: Bill, what in the world are you doing?

BILL: What does it look like, Whitney?

WHITNEY: It looks like you're *trying* to dance.

BILL: There's no *trying* going on here—you wish you had these moves.

WHITNEY: Maybe I can help you. There is a dance school right here in New York City *(Bill mutters, ''Not me. I don't need a dance school.'')* Like I was saying, there is a dance school in Harlem. Its members have traveled all over the world. Our next award will be presented in the field of dance. And presenting that award is someone who knows a step or two himself. Singer, movie star, dancer, and now appearing as Jelly Roll Morton on Broadway—Gregory Hines!

GREGORY: The Shining Star Award is presented to an innovative, creative, renowned dancer who founded the Dance Theater of Harlem in 1969. He was headed for Brazil to further his dancing career when the assassination of Dr. Martin Luther King affected him so tremendously that it changed his whole perspective. He wanted to serve his people as Dr. King had done by bringing ballet to the African American community. He opened The Dance Theater of Harlem in 1969.

Today The Dance Theater of Harlem is one of the most highly respected leaders worldwide in the field of dance. This Shinning Star is presented to Arthur Mitchell—founder of The Dance Theater of Harlem.

ARTHUR :MITCHELL: Thank you Gregory. Dr. King did inspire me as he did the world. People said the African American body was not built for the intricate movement of ballet. They said African Americans could never be great ballet dancers. Dr. King inspired me to believe that all things are possible. A great African American woman said these wise words: Don't limit yourself because of others' limited imagination and never limit another because of your limited imagination. Thank you very much for this award. And now I present to you my dance company performing a ballet, Pachebelle [Pa-Ka-bell] Canon. The Dance Theater of Harlem!

(Curtains open—Dancers perform)

WHITNEY: Our next award is given to an outstanding athlete. Presenting the Shining Star in the field of sports is *(Whitney and Bill say together):* Arseniooooooooooooo Hall!

ARSENIO: The Shilling Star award in the field of sports goes to one of the most incredible basketball players of our time—Michael Jordan. Michael Jordan was cut from his high school team—now that makes me go "mmmmm"—how does that high school coach feel now. Number 23 Jordan leaps high in the sky like a beautiful bird—which earned him the nickname Air Jordan. He led his team the Chicago Bulls to NBA Championships as well as winning a Gold Medal at the 1992 Olympics as a member of the famous Dream Team. He is the hero to many aspiring young people who he spends much of his spare time speaking to stressing the importance of hard work, perseverance, and the importance of an education. The Shining Star is presented to Michael Jordan.

JORDAN: Thank you Arsenio for bringing up that I was cut from my high school basketball team. I was cut but with determination I came back and with practice and hard work I succeeded. And you can do it whether it be in sports or in your education. Thank you for this special award.

BILL: Our next category is the field of business. Presenting that award is director/producer of motion pictures like "Do The Right Thing," "Jungle Fever," "School Daze" and the highly acclaimed "Malcolm X"—He's Mr. Spike Lee.

SPIKE: The recipient of the Shining Star Award in business can definitely be called the queen of television talk shows. Born in Kosciusko, Mississippi, she credits her father Vernon Winfrey, a barber and city councilman, as the person who saved her life. The Oprah Winfrey Show, which first aired in 1985 has won over eight Emmys and four NAACP Image Awards. Oprah Winfrey became the first African American woman to host a nationally syndicated weekday talk show. Oprah's ability to handle controversial topics with personal warmth has made her one of the wealthiest women in the country. Because of this success she was able to form her own production company called Harpo Productions and bought her own show. Oprah won an Academy Award for her portrayal as Sophia in the movie "The Color Purple." Her company has produced many television movies which tried to portray truthful images of African American life. Congratulations, Oprah—you are a shining star!

OPRAH: I am grateful and blessed because those women whose names made the history books and a lot who did not are all bridges that I've crossed over to get to where I am today. I am the product of every other black woman before me who has done or said anything worthwhile. Recognizing that I am a part of history is what allows me to soar.

WHITNEY: Our next Shining Star will be given to the entertainer of the year. Here to present that award are two shining stars themselves—she's a dancer, singer, actress—star of "It's A Different World"—you know her as Whitley but she's really Jasmine Guy, and, comedian, actor, and sometimes singer Eddie Murphy.

JASMINE: Our next recipient is a dynamic individual. Born in Gary, Indiana, he and his brothers were signed to Motown as The Jackson Five-Five brothers who took the music world by storm.

EDDIE: The success of the Jackson Five was phenomenal, but Michael soon launched his solo career producing hit after hit, gold albums, stacking up hundreds of awards. During his career Michael still finds time to reach out and help others. His generous donations to the United Negro College Fund, gives deserving African Americans the opportunity to pursue a college career.

JASMINE: He is the founder of Heal The World Foundation which works to save our environment and promote peace and harmony among all people of the world.

EDDIE: Most recently Michael's private jets have transported loads of food to war torn Sarejevo, and to the starving people of Somalia. His hard work, energy and talent coupled with love and concern for his fellow man has created an unprecedented global love. Michael Jackson, your success is truly an American Dream come true.

JASMINE: And you are truly a Shining Star—The award goes to Michael Jackson!

MICHAEL: I thank all of you, I love you.

EDDIE: That Michael Jackson, he just talks and talks and talks. Never shuts up. Performing the title song from the record breaking album "Thriller"—is Michael Jackson!

(Michael Jackson performs).

WHITNEY: Bill it's been a wonderful evening and you've been a wonderful co-host.

BILL: It sure has Whitney and until next year—keep these words in mind—A people must use its own talents, take pride in their own history, and love its own memories, then and only then can they become a better instrument for living together harmoniously with other people. Goodnight!

(Music: "HEAL THE WORLD")

THE END

copyright 1995

CHAPTER 12—

SOURCES

Works Cited:
BLACK HISTORY FIGURES

BOOKER T. WASHINGTON   (WIKIPEDIA.ORG)

W.E.B. DUBOIS   (WIKIPEDIA.ORG)

HARRIET TUBMAN   (WIKIPEDIA.ORG)

ABRAHAM LINCOLN   (WIKIPEDIA.ORG)

SHAKA THE GREAT   (UNESCO COLLECTION, AFRICAN
                             AUTHOR SERIES)

EMANCIPATION PROCLAMATION   (U.S. NATIONAL ARCHIVES)

MARCUS GARVEY   (WIKIPEDIA.ORG; AFRICA WITHIN.COM)

GRANVILLE T. WOODS   (WIKIPEDIA.ORG)

JACKIE ROBINSON   (WIKIPEDIA.ORG)

LANGSTON HUGHES   (WIKIPEDIA.ORG)

GARRETT MORGAN   (WIKIPEDIA.ORG; ABOUT.COM)

MAYA ANGELOU   (MAYA ANGELOU OFFICIAL WEB SITE)

CARTER G. WOODSON   (THE ASALH WEB SITE)

MANSA MUSA   (WIKIPEDIA.ORG)

BENJAMIN BANNEKER   (WIKIPEDIA.ORG)

THURGOOD MARSHALL   (WIKIPEDIA.ORG)

SHIRLEY SHISHOLM   (WIKIPEDIA.ORG)

JESSEE JACKSON   (WIKIPEDIA.ORG)

MAYNARD JACKSON   (WIKIPEDIA.ORG)

EDWARD BROOKE   (WIKIPEDIA.ORG)

CARL STOKES   (WIKIPEDIA.ORG)

COLEMAN YOUNG   (WIKIPEDIA.ORG)

MALCOLM X   (WIKIPEDIA.ORG)

MARTIN LUTHER KING, JR   (WIKIPEDIA.ORG)

ROSA PARKS	(WIKIPEDIA.ORG)
LEWIS LATIMER	(WIKIPEDIA.ORG)
GEORGE WASHINGTON CARVER	(WIKIPEDIA.ORG)
SOJOURNER TRUTH	(WIKIPEDIA.ORG)